NUMBERING THE CRIME

Forensic Mathematics

THE CRIME SCENE CLUB: FACT AND FICTION

NUMBERING THE CRIME

Forensic Mathematics

Kenneth McIntosh

Mason Crest Publishers

Numbering the Crime: Forensic Mathematics

MASON CREST PUBLISHERS INC.
370 Reed Road
Broomall, Pennsylvania 19008
(866)MCP-BOOK (toll free)
www.masoncrest.com

First Printing

9 8 7 6 5 4 3 2 1

ISBN 978-1-4222-0259-3 (series)

Library of Congress Cataloging-in-Publication Data

McIntosh, Kenneth, 1959–
 Numbering the crime : forensic mathematics / by Kenneth McIntosh.
    p. cm. — (The Crime Scene Club)
 Includes bibliographical references and index.
 ISBN 978-1-4222-0257-9   ISBN 978-1-4222-1460-2
 [1. Criminal investigation—Fiction. 2. Forensic sciences—Fiction. 3. Mystery and detective stories.] I. Title.
 PZ7.M1858Num 2009
 [Fic]—dc22
                        2008039813

Design by MK Bassett-Harvey.
Produced by Harding House Publishing Service, Inc.
www.hardinghousepages.com
Cover design by MK Bassett-Harvey.
Cover and interior illustrations by John Ashton Golden.
Printed in Malaysia.

CONTENTS

INTRODUCTION

The sound of breaking glass. A scream. A shot. Then . . . silence. Blood, fingerprints, a bullet, a skull, fire debris, a hair, shoeprints—enter the wonderful world of forensic science. A world of searching to find clues, collecting that which others cannot see, testing to find answers to seemingly impossible questions, and testifying to juries so that justice will be served. A world where curiosity, love of a puzzle, and gathering information are basic. The books in this series will take you to this world.

The CSI Effect

The TV show *CSI: Crime Scene Investigator* became so widely popular that *CSI: Miami* and *CSI: NY* followed. This forensic interest spilled over into *Bones* (anthropology); *Crossing Jordan* and *Dr. G* (medical examiners); *New Detectives* and *Forensic Files*, which cover all the forensic disciplines. Almost every modern detective story now involves forensic science. Many fiction books are written, some by forensic scientists such as Kathy Reichs (anthropology) and Ken Goddard (criminalistics and crime scene), as well as textbooks such as *Criminalistics* by Richard Saferstein. Other crime fiction authors are Sir Arthur Conan Doyle (Sherlock Holmes), Thomas Harris (*Red Dragon*), Agatha Christie (Hercule Poirot) and Ellis Peters, whose hero is a monk, Cadfael, an ex-Crusader who solves crimes. The list goes on and on—and I encourage you to read them all!

The spotlight on forensic science has had good *and* bad effects, however. Because the books and TV shows are so enjoyable, the limits of science have been blurred to make the plots more interesting. Often when students are intrigued by the TV shows and want to learn more, they have a rude awakening. The crime scene investigators on TV do the work of many professionals, including police officers, medical examiners, forensic laboratory scientists, anthropologists, and entomologists, to mention just a few. And all this in addition to processing crime scenes! Fictional instruments give test results at warp speed, and crimes are solved in forty-two minutes. Because of the overwhelming popularity of these shows, juries now expect forensic evidence in every case.

The books in this series will take you to both old and new forensic sciences, perhaps tweaking your interest in a career. If so, take courses in chemistry, biology, math, English, public speaking, and drama. Get a summer job in a forensic laboratory, courthouse, law enforcement agency, or an archeological dig. Seek internships and summer jobs (even unpaid). Skills in microscopy, instrumentation, and logical thinking will help you. Curiosity is a definite plus. You must read and understand procedures; take good notes; calculate answers; and prepare solutions. Public speaking and/or drama courses will make you a better speaker and a better expert witness. The ability to write clear, understandable reports aimed at nonscientists is a must. Salaries vary across the country and from agency to agency. You will never get rich, but you will have a satisfying, interesting career.

So come with me into this wonderful world called forensic science. You will be intrigued and entertained. These books are awesome!

—Carla M. Noziglia MS, FAAFS

Chapter 1
TRAPPED

All my life I've been told, "Don't open the door to strangers"—but how can it hurt this once?

When Jessa Carter answered the doorbell, she was greeted with a cheerful but phony-sounding recitation: "Hi. I'm Heather, and I'm competing in a contest to earn money for college and win a trip to Disneyland. I'm selling discount subscriptions of all kinds—we have *CosmoGirl*, *Seventeen*, and *Girls' Life* magazines."

Jessa contemplated the young woman on the other side of the screen door. She had bright purple hair cut close to the neck in back. Her eyebrows and ears were covered with piercings.

"*CosmoGirl*? Gag me." Jessa instantly felt bad, seeing the crestfallen look on the girl's face. "Sorry, didn't mean to be rude. I'm just not into the lipstick and fashion thing. My name's Jessa, by the way. Do you sell *Progressive* ? Or *The Nation*?"

"Just a minute." The girl glanced at a paper in her hand.

Jessa noticed the sweat dripping off the girl's brow. "Wicked hot out today."

"No kidding. I'm just about ready to pass out."

Jessa unlatched the screen door and opened it just an inch. "Why don't you come in and chill for a while? I have fresh-made iced tea, and you look like you need a rest."

Almost as soon as the words left her mouth, Jessa kicked herself mentally. Sure, the young woman on the doorstep looked innocent enough—but after a year in Crime Scene Club, Jessa knew that lots of people were far from what they seemed.

Maybe I'm just feeling lonely. Her friends were in Acapulco for the senior class trip. She had decided not to go, partly because she enjoyed time alone— painting, writing poetry, walking in the woods— and partly because she didn't want to struggle to come up with the $1,800 needed for the trip. She had seen the others off with a smile, but now, three days later, she was tired of her own company.

Or maybe I'm letting her in because she looks like Maeve. Granted, she radiated a different sort of attitude. Jessa's friend Maeve was always angry with the world, and made her peers cower in her presence. Heather, by contrast, seemed to have been run over by life's truck, all eighteen wheels. Jessa was afraid if she touched the girl, she might cry. Yet Heather had the same conforming-to-nonconformity style that Maeve had, and similar big brown eyes that said, *You really can trust me.*

Mostly, Jessa offered the invitation out of simple kindness. This girl on the doorstep was trying to be chipper—to make a sale she probably needed desperately—but she was obviously tired, depressed, sweaty, and miserable. Jessa opened the screen door wider. "Come on in, relax a minute."

The girl looked furtively to both sides.

She's scared, Jessa thought.

"I really shouldn't."

"It's all right—I don't bite." Jessa smiled. "And I'm not going to serve you drugs baked in brownies. I might look like an earth-mother but I swear I'm totally straight edge."

The girl glanced nervously to both sides again, then said, "Okay. Thanks," and stepped inside.

Jessa gestured to the couch and went into the kitchen. "The tea's a little bitter. You want sugar added?"

"Yeah, that'd be great."

Jessa came back in the living room with two cold glasses, handed one to her guest, and sat in an old rocking chair that faced the couch. She pointed to a plate full of oatmeal cookies on the coffee table between them. "Just made those. Not good for my shape—shouldn't be pigging out like this—but they're really good."

The girl smiled shyly, took a cookie, and pointed at the sketches and paintings that hung on the wall. "Nice art."

"Thanks." Jessa grinned. "Those are pieces I did this year for school."

"Wow. You're talented!"

"Thanks."

Heather's gaze fixed on a sketch of a young man with long dark hair, high cheekbones, and a piercing gaze. "Good looking guy. Is that a real person?"

Jessa hesitated. "That's my . . . former boy-friend."

"But you still have his picture on the wall?"

"Yeah, it's . . . complicated."

Heather changed the subject. "So what were those magazines you wanted? They were ones I don't usually hear mentioned." She shuffled through her papers.

"You're not from here, are you?" Jessa smiled. "Those are about the most popular magazines in these parts."

"Yeah, I'm from Chicago."

"Long way from home. Been on the road long?"

Heather nodded. "Seems like forever."

"So, how you like selling magazines? Is it a cool job?"

"Yeah, sure. It's the greatest."

Wow, Jessa thought, *that's the least sincere-sounding answer I've ever heard*. Something about Heather's tone made Jessa want to probe deeper. "Really, is it that great—or is that what they train you to say?"

The young woman pursed her lips.

"I'm just offering a shoulder to cry on," Jessa said softly, "'cause you don't exactly look like a happy camper."

Heather sighed. She glanced around the room as if she were expecting the shadows to jump out and attack her.

Jessa waited. She suspected this door-to-door waif was lugging along a very heavy burden.

"It sucks . . . totally," Heather told her finally, and then she let out an awkward laugh. "It's really, really bad."

"Then why do you do it?"

The brow beneath the purple hair wrinkled. "You're gonna think I'm a total loser," she said.

"Oh, no. Not me. I've been through a childhood full of crap you wouldn't believe—and the past year from hell to top it all off." In her mind's eye, Jessa flashed through memories: her beloved art teacher murdered, along with her own near-death by poisoning. "Believe me, Heather, I'm all ears and no judgment."

After hesitating a moment, the girl on the couch explained, "It's awful work but if you could see my life before . . ."

"Not all sunshine, huh?"

Heather shook her head. "I grew up in a totally ghetto part of the city. If we could've afforded to live anywhere else—anywhere in the world—we would've. But Mom isn't so smart. I swear, if she ever made a right choice in life she'd die of shock. School wasn't exactly fun. You can't make it if you don't join a gang there."

"And I'm guessing you didn't."

"No way. I'm my own person, even if it means getting my lunch taken every day—and the snot beat out of me every couple of weeks."

Jessa grimaced. "Did you make it through school?"

"Nope. Couldn't take it. Dropped out last year, when I was a junior."

"I don't know if I could stay in, with that kind of pressure," Jessa told her. "What did you do after school?"

"Worked a couple jobs, but honest employment in my 'hood wasn't any better than school was."

Jessa nodded sympathetically.

"Then, one day this guy comes to the door selling magazines. He had a big bright smile and he talked a mile-a-minute. I figured he was schmoozing, but still . . . he had style. 'At least this dude is alive,' I told myself. And I could tell he liked me—and honestly, I was more than a little interested in him, too. So he says I could come with him, and we'd have a great time on his sales crew. He talked about traveling all over the place—seeing the ocean and amusement parks and all the pretty little towns on the way. Said I'd make all kinds of money. We could party every night, too."

"It looked like a really attractive way out," Jessa agreed.

"It did. I left my mom a note on the table, threw some clothes in a duffle bag, grabbed my purse, and off we went—the start of my whole new crappy life." Heather shook her head.

"How long you been at this?"

"Seven months now. At first, it was pretty much the way he promised it would be. They taught me all the right things to say and started me in a decent suburb where there were good pickings and it was safe. I was the only girl on the crew, and that was good for them, because folks get a bit scared seeing some dude at their door. I can be all cutesy and sweet—so I was top-seller on the crew for the first few weeks. Then, it got harder. We sold in some places that weren't so good. Couple of times, dirty old men tried to grab me. Other folks would be all over my face, yelling at me and stuff. We worked from first thing in the morning till late at night, seven days a week, in the rain and the snow even. It is so exhausting. Then Jerald—that's the guy that came to my door—he got traded to another sales crew, and he didn't seem at all broke up about it. So I guess he just used me, and he's probably all sweet on the next girl now."

"So it isn't the dream job you thought it would be."

Heather shook her head. "It gets worse—lots worse. Pretty soon they teach you how to take advantage of people. If someone signs up for one magazine, you check off three or four more."

Jessa laughed "I'm glad I didn't buy from you."

"So am I. Really. I'm by no means perfect, but I never set out to take advantage of people. The stuff I do every day, it makes me hate myself—but you have to pull tricks like that, or the managers take it out on you. If you don't sell enough during the day, they make you do a hundred pushups, or drink water with spit in it and crap like that. Then on really bad days—when we don't make enough sales to cover the hotel and meals—they just keep the money and throw away the filled order forms."

"So the people you sell to don't get the magazines they ordered?"

"A lot of times they just get their money taken."

"And your managers know this?"

"Oh, our managers. There's this couple that runs our crew: Bonnie and Dylan. Dylan is all right, least most of the time. But Bonnie. . ." Heather shook her head. "At first I admired her, because she looked like everything I want to be. She's tough, but not in a cheap way. I've met lots of girls act all brassy but you know that's because they're really scared on the inside. Not Bonnie. She's her own woman—intimidated by no one. She's smart, looks good, doesn't take any crap or get her feathers ruffled. And besides, she warmed right up to me. Took me under her wing, said she hoped someday she'd have a daughter like me—all kinds of manure."

"Lies, huh?"

"Nothing but. Pretty soon, she was pressuring me—saying I was falling behind in sales, had to make more and more."

"Were you making less than when you started?"

"No way. Bonnie was just screwing with my head—trying to make a bigger profit. And she kept pressuring me to drink and get high with the other kids."

"But that's illegal."

"No duh. There's so much wrong about this outfit—you haven't heard the half of it. They're too cheap to get us decent rooms, so we stay at these total dives. Bonnie and Dylan get their own room—usually the best one there is. Then, me and two guys get the cheapest, usually a single bed—and the person with the least sales each day gets to sleep on the floor."

"That's awful."

"Oh, the floor's not so bad. Sometimes I under-report, because I want to sleep on the ground. That way I don't have to put up with a drunken boy trying to grope me all night."

Jessa shook her head so hard her dreadlocks whipped back and forth. "Why don't you report that to your supervisors?"

"You kidding? You think Bonnie and Dylan *care*? Don't you see—they want to treat us bad. It's the way you keep slaves in line."

"Is that how it feels—like you're a slave?"

"Totally. Things keep getting worse, so by now they're treating me and the guys like we're just their servants. They insist we party every night—but they supply all the booze and the pot, and they charge us way too much for that stuff. So we have to take out loans. All that talk about getting rich and seeing Disneyland and stuff? No way. Fact is, I'm a thousand dollars in the hole. I totally owe those guys." Heather lowered her voice to a whisper. "Bonnie is like this monster that runs the whole operation—the whole crew is scared of her, even her husband."

"Why don't you call your mom and go home, Heather? This isn't a marketing group, this is like—a cult. Next thing you know they're going to mix up a pot of Kool-Aid and cyanide."

"I could believe that. But. . ." She twisted a purple strand of hair around her finger. "We used to have this guy on our crew, Trevor. He was nice, funny—and he wouldn't go along with it all. He told us he was leaving. And one day, he just disappeared. I thought he'd gone home, like he said. That's what Dylan and Bonnie told us. But another guy on the crew—he told us a different story. Said Dylan and Bonnie paid him to lure Trevor into an alley, while he was on his sales route one day. Dylan held his hands behind his back, and Bonnie went at him with a bat. This guy that told me—said he was watching from around the corner. Said they beat Trevor so bad, you wouldn't believe it. Then they rolled him up in a plastic sheet and took off with him in the back of the van. The guy who saw it couldn't even say if he was still alive."

Jessa sucked in a breath. "So you're scared to leave."

"You would be too."

Jessa nodded, then said slowly, "Listen, I have friends—contacts with the police department in town. If I make a call, I can get Detective Kwan over here in minutes. She's the greatest—like super-woman. She can shoot, kick, climb walls—but she really cares about people, too. She saved my life. I mean, literally."

Heather shook her head. "I can't rat on them. They'd find me."

"My friends can keep you safe. For real. I promise."

Heather was shaking. "No way. I can't. I shouldn't have told you all this stuff."

Jessa leaned toward her. "Let me call for help, Heather. You have to get away from this crew."

Heather was hyperventilating now, Jessa realized.

"I haven't. . . There's more I haven't told you."

"So tell me."

"The worst thing about this crew is. . . They don't want a soul to know that—"

Before she could say anything more, a loud knock sounded on the screen door: *bam-bam-bam!*

Both young women jumped. A stocky man stood outside. "Anybody home?" he shouted as he squinted through the screen.

Jessa put a finger to her lips, pointed toward the back of the house, and gestured for Heather to follow. Before they could move, though, the man opened the door and stepped inside.

"Hey!" Jessa screamed.

"I'm looking for this chick here." The man pointed at Heather.

Must be Dylan, Jessa thought. "Get out of my house or I'll call the police and have you arrested."

He shook his head. "Not if you can't get to the phone."

Jessa turned to Heather. "Run—out the back door!"

Heather didn't hesitate. The man lunged after her, but Jessa swung a leg in front of his shin. He stumbled, fell onto his knee.

"You stupid—" Dylan's eyes blazed with anger as he struggled to his feet, but Jessa's foot caught him with a roundhouse kick in the side of the face. He fell back against the coffee table, smashing its glass surface with his elbow. He lay in a disheveled pile on the living room floor, moaning.

Jessa dashed out the back door.

Whumpf.

Jessa was suddenly on her back. Someone had grabbed her hand and flipped her hard on the concrete of the patio—so fast she barely perceived the motion. The same someone stood over her with a stiletto heel lightly touching Jessa's windpipe.

Groaning, Jessa looked up the length of a sleek pantsuit, into a woman's roundish face below smooth blond hair. The woman was smiling; she'd look rather pleasant, Jessa mused, were she not holding her heel on Jessa's throat.

"Hello. I'm Bonnie. I don't believe we've met."

Jessa groaned. Her shoulder had taken the fall—thank goodness it wasn't the back of her head. *She got me by surprise, Jessa thought. But I have a few surprises myself—like three years of Hapkido.*

Quick as a cat, Jessa rolled and swept an arm at the woman's leg. She failed to connect, but managed to stand. For a second they faced one another. Then—

The woman punched her in the ribs—before Jessa could even begin to block. Jessa doubled over.

Wham. The woman threw Jessa face forward onto the pavement. Now she really hurt. *Okay, remind me not to mess with business-suit karate woman.*

Click. Jessa felt cold steel on her hands; she was being cuffed. Then she heard the sound of duct tape zipping off a roll, and before she could scream, the sticky stuff wound around her head, gagging her mouth shut.

The sound of an opening door told Jessa the man had come out of the house. "Oh, Dylan," the woman said, "I wondered where you were. I can't believe you let two little girls get the best of you. What ever would you do if I weren't around to rescue your sorry butt?"

She yanked Jessa to her feet. For an instant, Jessa considered running, but then thought better. She decided to save energy for a chance to escape later—when they were unsuspecting, and she wasn't in so much pain. Heather, likewise cuffed and taped, stood beside her.

"Dylan," the woman commanded, "pull the van back here so we won't attract attention."

He muttered an assent, and a minute later, a big rust-red van backed into the yard. Bonnie swung the back gate open and shoved the two young women inside. Dylan walked back to them, grabbed their cuffed hands, and wrapped a thick bicycle-lock chain around the cuffs and into eyelets that were welded onto the interior wall of the van.

Shackled. These people don't mess around. As the van's motor started, Jessa realized no one would know who took her. She saw no way to escape, and little hope of rescue.

Meanwhile, Ken Benally, Jessa's ex-boyfriend, was thinking, *I still think they put me in the wrong class.* The words on the book cover—*Mathematical Probabilities, Predictions and Analysis of Criminal Case*s—were beginning to blur. Ken shut his eyes and rubbed them. He leaned back in his swivel chair and spun it away from the dorm desk where the book lay amid a pile of notebooks.

"I so hate math," he mumbled to himself. He'd had a rough first year at Northern Arizona University; he had not made many friends, and even though he'd done well in his high school coursework, the classes at NAU seemed overwhelming. Especially this class in mathematical forensics. He was utterly befuddled by lectures on hypothesis testing, algorithms, neural networks, and Bayesian analysis. It all looked great on that television show where Charlie Eppes, the CalSci professor, helped the FBI solve criminal cases every week. But that was more like a soap opera than the stuff Ken had to try and learn in class.

He wanted to do well in his courses, especially the forensics ones. His father, Sergeant Victor Benally of the Flagstaff Police Department, had—intentionally or not—set the course of Ken's future career. His parents divorced before he started high school, and since then his home life was an unrelenting atmosphere of male toughness and crime-fight talk. Partly, Ken wanted to follow his father's footsteps because he saw him as a twenty-first–century warrior, an heir to the proud tradition of their Navajo heritage. The other motivation pushing Ken toward police work was Crime Scene Club, the group he had belonged to his senior year in high school. Under the leadership of Detective Dorothy Kwan, the team of students had cracked several real cases. In one mystery, Ken had rescued his own mother from a gang of art thieves. CSC had provided some of the scariest—but also the most fulfilling—moments of Ken's life.

So now, in his freshman year at NAU, Ken was doggedly determined to succeed in the study of criminology. Unfortunately, that meant passing this mathematics course—and he didn't feel very confident about that right now. Thankfully, he had help from Wire, the science genius member of Crime Scene Club. Wire could be condescending— "That's so obvious, man, how come you don't get it?"—but Ken appreciated his tutoring. It was his only chance to make it through math.

As he sighed and turned back to the desk, Ken's eyes fell on the photo propped at the back of his desk: blue eyes, matted hair under a Jamaican knit cap, pouty lips, and rosy cheeks.

Jessa.

They'd dated since his freshmen year, and she had been the fixed point to Ken's compass—his muse, companion, lover, and best friend in the world. But some twisted spot in Ken's soul had messed everything up. He had been unfaithful. First he found himself kissing Lupe Arellano, another member of CSC. Then he had that brief fling with Veronika, a former *American Idol* star who had been involved in one of the CSC cases. And on top of that, he had sort of asked Lupe for a date while he was feeling lonely over the summer.

Now, finally, after all that confusion with girls, he knew what he wanted. All along, despite the fog of hormones and twisted emotions, he had only desired one thing. To share his life with Jessa.

And that could have been his life, even now. *Except*, Ken told himself, *I'm an idiot.*

As Ken watched the other guys in his dorm and their dating lives, he recognized himself all too well. Girls were conquests; guys were players. Ken had thought he truly cared about the various women in his life—but all along, he'd really only cared about what felt good at the moment.

He had blown it. The consequences of his own choices woke up with him every lonely morning, sat with him through every lonely meal, and lay with him every lonely night.

He glanced at the wall clock: one in the afternoon. *What is she doing now?* he wondered. Their mutual friend Maeve had told him that Jessa stayed behind while the rest of their CSC friends went on the senior trip. Was she hiking through a pass on the San Francisco Peaks, just outside of town? Was she painting in her makeshift studio? Or sitting on her couch, strumming her well-worn Martin guitar?

As he thought more about Jessa, Ken's mind flooded with memories of her touch, the smell of her perfume, the sound of her voice. He was flooded with conviction: final exams coming up or not, he had to try again. He had to see her. Throw himself on her mercy. Declare what a fool he had been and beg her to re-start their relationship.

He grabbed his truck keys and wallet and headed for the parking lot.

Chapter 2
NEEDLE IN A HAYSTACK

The neighborhood, bathed in sunlight, seemed peaceful and still as he parked in front of Jessa's home. He took a deep breath and rubbed his fingers over a fetish in a pouch around his neck. The elders were skeptical that spiritual medicine could do much for lovesickness. A botched relationship was the result of human disharmony and could only be fixed by freewill and wise choices. Still, a bit of luck couldn't hurt.

The wooden inner door was open, so someone was home. He didn't see Mrs. Carter's old station wagon in the driveway, so he guessed Jessa would be the only one there. Feeling as though his legs were wobbling beneath him, he walked to the door, tapped on the screen, and waited.

No one answered.

"Jessa?" he called.

The only answer this time was a meow from the cat, somewhere inside.

Ken put his eye up to the screen and squinted through the dim interior light. He saw no one. Then something he could see made him suck in his breath: broken glass in the middle of the floor.

He put his hand on the button of the latch; the door was unlocked. "Jessa?" he called again, louder. His guts were giving him a clear message: *Something is terribly wrong*. He waited another minute, then opened the door and stepped inside.

He called again as he stepped around the mess in the living room to look in the rest of the house: the living room, kitchen, Jessa's room, her mother's room, and a small studio. No one home anywhere.

When he glanced out the back door, he saw tire tracks on the back lawn. His uneasy feeling grew worse. He didn't recall Jessa or her mom ever parking there.

Ken turned back toward the front of the house, and—

A woman screamed.

He jumped, then saw who stood in the doorway and let out his breath in relief.

"Ken Benally! What on earth are you doing here?"

"I am so sorry, Mrs. Carter. I can explain." He spoke so fast he was forgetting to breathe. "I came to see Jessa, and the door was unlocked and I saw the mess in the family room, and I thought I'd better investigate. I didn't mean to trespass in your house, I swear."

Mrs. Carter had always impressed Ken as an older, stouter version of Jessa: the same kind eyes, same forgiving, and wise soul. She threw up her hands. "Goodness, Ken. You don't have to go on. I believe you. But I'm worried. Where could Jessa be?"

"Did she say she was going anywhere today?"

The woman shook her head. "No. In fact, we planned to meet now for afternoon tea. She said she'd make cookies, and it looks like she did." Mrs. Carter pointed to a half-dozen oatmeal pastries strewn among the broken remains of the coffee table. "We were going to hang out. She wanted to read me some poems she's been working on." Her lips tightened, as though she were determined to hold back her emotion.

"We need to call the police," Ken said. "I–I'm afraid something's happened here."

Mrs. Carter nodded.

Ken knew his father was out of town on a case, so he punched the speed dial for Detective Kwan. She was at her office doing paperwork, and as soon as Ken explained the circumstance, she promised to come quickly.

Minutes later, three squad cars pulled up: Detective Kwan and a detachment of officers. She spoke briefly with Ken and Mrs. Carter, looked at the floor, and then agreed there was cause for concern. "Please step away from the middle of the room, and try not to touch anything," she requested.

An officer stooped by the broken coffee table. "There are traces of blood on the wood and glass here, detective."

"Take samples." She squinted at the floor. "That cookie looks half eaten. Think we can get DNA off that?"

"We can try."

Ken wanted to say something to the detective, away from Jessa's mother so they wouldn't upset her. "Detective, there's something out back you should see."

She nodded and they stepped into the backyard. Ken pointed out the odd tire marks, and Detective Kwan spied a single earring, turquoise in a silver setting, lying on the concrete. She bent down, picked it up with a pair of tweezers.

"I recognize that—it's Jessa's," Ken told her.

"The loop has been twisted, and there's a tiny red spot here," Detective Kwan noted.

"Looks like something that would happen if there was a struggle," Ken said quietly.

Detective Kwan nodded and then replied in an equally subdued tone, "Consistent with the scene in the house. I'm guessing—it's only a preliminary observation, mind you—that someone entered through the unlocked screen door. The intruder and Jessa struggled in the living room, then again here. The intruder or an accomplice pulled their vehicle onto the back lawn, and. . ." She paused, clearly unwilling to finish.

Ken tried to hold his voice steady as he finished her thought: "Then the assailant drove away with Jessa."

Dorothy Kwan nodded. "I'm afraid we'd better treat this as an abduction."

Ken crouched down for a moment to steady himself. Black dots danced in front of his eyes.

"Do you know of any case that she was working on?" Ms. Kwan asked.

"No. Maeve said Jessa stayed in town this week to work on her art stuff."

"Can you think of anyone with a grudge against her?"

"You probably know that better than I do. Prakash hasn't been seen since the devil dog poisoning case—but I think he and Jessa were friends even after what happened. The Anaconda workers were awfully mad at her for a while, but then they switched sides and supported her work for Lewis Henry. She's always had adolescent groupies, from the time we had the band. But none of them ever threatened violence—it was just puppy-love stuff." He shook his head. "I can't think of any real enemies who would do this."

"That's pretty much what I know, too," Ms. Kwan agreed.

"Maeve and Lupe are in Acapulco. Should we call them?" Ken asked.

The detective hesitated, then shook her head. "No. They can't do anything from there. They're on a cruise and it would probably take a few days to arrange transportation back to the States. Since they can't help, and they spent all that money for the trip. . ." She forced a smile. "Anyway, by the time they return we'll have Jessa back safe and sound."

"I hope so." Ken had a sudden thought. "Think we should call Wire?"

"I'll have an officer track him down, get him on the case ASAP."

"Good."

Detective Kwan put her hand on Ken's shoulder. "Have faith. Jessa's tough—she'll know how to handle herself in this situation. We'll have a solid team working nonstop till she's found. We just need to keep our wits about us and everything will turn out okay."

Ken nodded, wishing he could believe her.

"I'd better ask Mrs. Carter some questions and check up on the team." Ms. Kwan turned back toward the house. "Time is—"

"I know," Ken interrupted. "Don't say it."

Ken was left alone in the backyard struggling with his emotions. Jessa Baby, where in the world are you? If he hadn't been such an utter idiot, maybe they would have been together this afternoon, and maybe this wouldn't have happened. He felt sick and frightened and angry. Jessa was gone, seemingly vanished into thin air. There'd been a struggle. But with whom? Why? And where was she now? Was she injured, or— *Stop. Don't go there.*

"Ken Benally?" An officer poked his head out the door. "Detective Kwan says you need to see something."

As Ken entered the living room, he saw Detective Kwan crouched by the broken coffee table, holding a piece of paper in her gloved hand.

"What's that?" Ken asked.

"It says, 'Exclusive Subscription Group.' Looks like a ledger of magazine sales."

"So a salesperson was here?"

"Appears so."

"Does the person have a name on the paper?"

"First name only: Heather."

"Do you think it connects with Jessa somehow?"

Dorothy Kwan glanced back at the paper. "The last entry is for twelve months of *Progressive* magazine, and—yes. The subscriber is Jessa Carter."

Ken breathed a small sigh of relief. "So we have a start. We're looking for someone with a magazine sales crew."

Detective Kwan nodded. "I already have an officer questioning the neighbors—she might be able to give us more information. And I have a man calling the Exclusive Subscription Group to find out about a crew in this area."

Ken noticed the frustrated look on the face of Jessa's mom. "Why would a magazine sales person take my daughter?" she burst out.

"I'm afraid we can't answer that," Detective Kwan told her. "But we do have the start of a trail now."

An officer came in the front door and reported, "I've canvassed all the houses on both sides of this street. Only three have folks at home, and two of those reported nothing strange—only that a girl came by trying to sell magazines."

"That girl is now our number-one lead in the case," Dorothy Kwan replied. "Do you have a description?"

"Five foot six, short-cropped dyed hair—one person says pink and the other says purple—dark lipstick, piercings all over her face. Wearing a black tank top and blue jeans. One person says the young woman appeared nervous, the other said she appeared to be suffering from the heat. She was very sweaty."

"All right." Detective Kwan nodded. "We have a name, a description, and the name of a company—we need to follow up on all this quickly."

"One more thing," the reporting officer added, "the woman across the street didn't see the sales girl, but she did mention something else. There was a faded red van parked in front of this house, for just a few minutes."

"Do we have a license number? Make?" Ms. Kwan asked.

"Neither. It didn't seem important to the observer—she had no idea there was an . . . incident here."

While Detective Kwan radioed in an APB describing the young woman and the van, Ken noticed Mrs. Carter's furrowed brow. He put a hand on the older woman's shoulder. "Jessa's going to be fine. I've seen her in some tough spots on our CSC cases—she can handle pretty much anything."

"I know. She's a lot smarter and stronger than I was—no, than I am. But a mother can't help but worry."

Ken nodded. "Me too."

The other officer in the house had been on his phone and now reported back to Detective Kwan. "I've spoken with the headquarters for Exclusive Subscription Group."

"And?"

"They say there are three sales crews that could possibly be operating in Arizona at this time, but each crew works independently—so they can't tell us where any specific group is."

"Not very helpful. Did they provide cell numbers for each crew?"

"They did—I've followed up."

"And ?"

"One is in southern Utah. They claim they've been selling in Kanab all day. The second is in Vegas."

"And the third?"

"Won't answer the phone."

"They're the ones we want. Do we have a name?"

"Dylan and Bonnie Neymer."

"Good work. License number?"

"The company says they'd be renting a vehicle. They couldn't give me any specifics."

"Get me a statewide search of rental agencies for that name."

The officer nodded.

Detective Kwan turned to Jessa's mother. "This is a good start for a case, Mrs. Carter. Things are looking up."

Jessa's mother nodded, but she didn't seem comforted. Ken didn't blame her. *Finding that van is like finding a needle in a haystack.* He had written a term paper on kidnap cases, and he knew that with every passing minute a kidnap victim's life is in greater danger. *Oh, Jessa,* he thought, *please be all right.*

Chapter 3
DESPERATE TIMES

Jessa ached. Her wrists chafed against the cuffs, her bottom was sore from the hard steel of the van's vibrating floor, and the tape over her mouth itched and pulled at her skin. She would have paid every penny in her meager bank account to have a hand free for just a minute to scratch that itch.

She looked at Heather, chained to the side of the vehicle across from her. Their eyes met and exchanged mutual emotions: fear, anger, desperation.

Jessa had guessed from the beginning that they were in lethal danger. Bonnie and Dylan were not hiding their names or faces from Jessa; therefore, they weren't worried that the girls might testify against them. That could only mean they intended murder.

The radio was playing—a country music station—but she could make out voices over the music. Dylan was driving; Bonnie was in the passenger seat working nonchalantly on a crossword puzzle.

"Just what we needed," Dylan said bitterly, "a pair of rats to screw things up."

"Settle down," Bonnie told him. "You're starting to sound like my ex—whimping out, getting all panicky. The thing in life is, don't stress out. Tell yourself, 'I'm in control—not my circumstances.' Everything turns out fine when you remember who's the master."

Jessa had observed Bonnie only for the hour since they met, but she had already intuited a lot about the woman. She'd be willing to bet that Bonnie was abused at some point in life, and the experience had taught her to be tough, to never be a victim again. Jessa reflected that, oddly, she and Bonnie were alike in that way. Jessa could respect a survivor. But Bonnie had gone way too far. Like a song said, *You become the monster, so the monster cannot eat you.* Now, Bonnie was the abuser—and Jessa and Heather her victims.

So how could Jessa take control of the situation? Options seemed badly limited, with her hands cuffed and chained to the side of the vehicle. She turned her attention back to the conversation between her captors.

"We're going to have to miss our drop," Dylan said. "Too much heat with those two in back."

"Don't be an idiot," Bonnie retorted. "Eight grams. We don't deliver, we're toast."

Grams? Jessa's mind was clouded by the morning's events. *You don't sell magazines in grams.* Then she realized. Heather had started to tell her, "The

worst thing about this crew is. . . ," but she didn't get a chance to finish. Now, Jessa could finish the thought for her. *They're drug runners; the magazine sales are just a front for their real operation.* She also surmised that the kids on the sales crew didn't know this. Somehow, Heather had realized the truth—and this now put both their lives in peril.

"You're not afraid to stop in Kingman?" Dylan asked.

"For ten grand, I'm not afraid of anything," Bonnie retorted.

"What if the cops are looking for us? They probably know the girl's missing by now."

"That's *all* they know. But to be sure, we'll switch plates."

"What're we gonna do with those two?" Dylan asked.

"The kids in the other car think Heather went home—they don't suspect a thing."

"But we can't keep them forever."

"Of course not. We'll dispose of them—after we're over the state line into California."

"Where?"

"I know a dump just outside Barstow. It's been closed for years—no one would look there."

Jessa could hear uneasiness in Dylan's voice. Apparently, he was still uncomfortable with the notion of cold-blooded murder. There was a note of hesitation in his voice as he asked, "You gonna kill them now, or later?"

"We'll check into the hotel, like we told the kids. I don't want to make any deviations from our previous plans—looks suspicious. We'll check into the hotel, keep these little snots in our room. The crew will never know a thing."

"But, when do we . . . when are these two off our hands?" Dylan asked.

Jessa felt her palms getting sweaty.

"Wait until everyone's done partying and sleeping soundly. Then, two or three in the morning, we'll sneak out, off 'em and dump 'em in the waste site."

Jessa found it harder to breath.

Bonnie added, "*I'll* do them by myself, if it makes you feel better."

Jessa's heart pounded.

"Oh, crud!" Dylan exclaimed suddenly. "We're gonna run outta gas."

"Be cool. We'll hit Seligman in a few minutes. Fuel up there. Just a quick stop."

Jessa frantically sought for options. It was hard concentrating with aching muscles, clutching fear, and the increasing discomfort of her bladder. *Wish I hadn't drank that iced tea.*

Then she glimpsed a very faint glimmer of hope. She felt the van slow down, turn, and park. The engine stopped, and she saw Bonnie and Dylan's faces turn toward the back of the van.

"Mmmph, mmmph," Jessa groaned from the back of her throat and nodded her head toward her tightly crossed legs.

Bonnie and Dylan exchanged glances.

"Let her pee herself," Bonnie said.

"It'll smell up the van," Dylan protested.

Bonnie let out an exasperated sigh. "All right. After you've filled up and we switch plates, then pull up to the side by the restrooms. I'll let them pee—but one at a time, and take no chances." She reached into the glove compartment, pulled a pistol out, and slid the top back, cocking it.

Jessa grimaced. *When am I going to get a break?*

First, Dylan got out. Jessa heard the sound of gas pumping into the vehicle. After a few minutes— he must be paying, Jessa guessed—the van pulled up behind the back of the station, and she heard sounds outside the tailgate. *License plate switch. Clever.* Finally, Dylan again re-entered the van and drove it just a short distance before stopping again. Bonnie looked back, glared, and stepped out.

Showtime.

The grim-faced woman opened the rear gate, and Jessa blinked at the sudden exposure to bright daylight. "Potty break," her captor muttered. She unlocked Heather's cuffs. The girl pushed herself up on stiff legs, and the woman pressed her pistol close to the girl's head and nodded to the restroom door.

Heather hobbled toward the restroom; then Bonnie opened the door, and Jessa watched as she went inside with the young woman. The restroom door closed.

Jessa raced mentally through her options. She was no match for Bonnie, even when the older woman was unarmed. Now, with her muscles cramped, how could she hope to escape when her adversary was holding a gun? On the other hand, she didn't have to get far. If she could make it into the front of the service station, she'd be able to tear off the gag and scream for help, hide behind the counter, whatever. Her captors would probably drag her away again, but it would be enough to alert authorities—and get help on their trail.

It was a very slender thread of hope. The odds were certainly against her. Jessa knew an attempt to escape could mean that her life ended abruptly.

Right now.

And yet she might not have another chance to break free.

The restroom door opened, and Heather was thrust back inside the van and chained again. Bonnie waved the pistol at Jessa. "Okay, knot head, take a pee, but no funny business. I wouldn't have any bad feelings about pulling this trigger."

Heaven help me, Jessa thought, *I believe it.* She took a slow, deep breath through her nose and swung her aching legs over the back of the van onto the gravel. She stood and took a step toward the restroom door. Her feet tingled from being so cramped. Her captor walked right beside her, gun jabbing into her ribs.

Jessa reached for the lavatory door. Her heart raced. In a few more moments, she could be free. Or dead.

"Coffee?" Detective Kwan asked, as she poured herself a cup.

"Thanks, but I'm plenty awake." Ken had felt increasingly agitated during the past hour. They had departed from the Carter residence and established an operations command center here in Ms. Kwan's office, but not much else had happened. And the clock was ticking. . . .

An officer stuck his head in the door. "Detective, we have some updates."

"Go ahead," she instructed the messenger.

Finally, thought Ken.

"We have reports that the young woman— Heather—was selling door-to-door in Holbrook, yesterday morning and afternoon."

The detective nodded. "Good tip. Anything else?"

"We widened our search of rentals. A red van was checked out by Mr. Dylan Neymer, the day before yesterday, by Enterprise Rental in Albuquerque, New Mexico. It's a three-quarter-ton Chevy, with license plate"—he glanced at a paper in his hand—"Alpha-Zebra-Tango 5-1-3. "

"Great. Thanks."

"We also have Neymer's license, along with his wife's, online. I've already sent it to you."

"Very good work. We'll get an APB out for that vehicle and alert authorities to be on the look out for the couple. I'll also have searches done on their credit cards in case they use one." Detective Kwan picked up a phone and rattled off instructions, alerting authorities throughout the state of this new information.

As she did so, Ken heard a knock at the door. He looked through the glass window and saw a young man with long face, longer blond hair, and thick glasses. He smiled and swung open the door. "Hey, Wire—good to see you, man."

"Dude, happy to help." The CSC computer expert stepped into the office. "What's the situation?"

Ken explained what they knew about the case, as Wire tapped information into his PDA.

"Glad to see you, Wire," Ms. Kwan said as she put the phone back on its cradle. "We need all the help we can get."

"Seems like the next step is pretty simple," Wire noted.

Simple? Ken didn't see anything simple about it. *How can Wire be so flip when Jessa's life is in danger?*

"Of course we don't know what *will* happen, but it's a no-brainer to predict what's *likely*," the geek went on.

Through the fog of fear and tension, Ken's memory caught a familiar pattern. "You're talking about future probability analysis. That's on my final exam."

Wire smiled. "You *are* learning something at NAU. I thought you were there to score with the hotties in your dorm."

Ken scowled, "Right now, there's only one woman on earth that I'm—"

Wire cut him off. "Yes, it's time to apply some principles from our dear friend Thomas Bayes."

That name does sound familiar. What did he do?

Wire continued, "We look at the existent pattern and then calculate in the relative probabilities of Possibility A versus Possibility B regarding the kidnapper's route."

I saw this equation on the board in class—I think.

Detective Kwan was ahead of Ken. "They've established an apogee headed along Interstate 40, from Albuquerque to Holbrook to Flagstaff, taking a day for each transition."

"Obviously."

Obviously? Ken felt his face grow hot.

"So, we first have to factor A—they continue on course—versus B—they deviate," Wire went on.

"There's one point for B and that is the desire to throw off pursuit," Detective Kwan suggested.

Wire nodded. "But I can think of more factors for A. First, the likelihood that there is some extrinsic motivation for the course that they're on. I don't know what that might be, but there's probably a method to their establishing a route. Another factor is that the abductors are going to be a tad nervous lugging a hostage along, and that should limit their capacity for creative thinking—hence greater likelihood of continuing on a pre-set course."

"Hey, wait a minute, I'm remembering something," Ken blurted. "To estimate likelihood, the probability of observing X if A is true is divided by the likelihood of X if B is true."

Wire nodded. "Say, you did get something out of paying your thousand dollars per class."

"Don't know what the heck it means," Ken admitted.

"It means they're probably in Kingman about now," Wire declared.

"No way," Ken retorted. "You can't possibly know—"

"It's a no-brainer. The odds are two-to-one that they continue heading west on I-40, probably driving 75 miles an hour. It's 120 miles, and a neighbor

reported seeing this girl, Heather, about an hour and a half ago. So we calculate—"

"Detective Kwan," the intercom on her desk interrupted.

"Yes?"

"We have a report from Kingman. Gas station attendant a few minutes ago saw a red Chevy van, male driver. Stopped for gas. I know it's a long shot, but.—"

"Do we have the license?"

"Negative. But we have a security cam tape. It's on computer, so they sent it over on our request. You want to see?"

"Absolutely. Get it right to my mail." Detective Kwan sat and tapped on a keyboard, bringing the flat screen monitor to life.

"Right where I predicted," Wire whispered.

Man, what an ego. "There's probably a thousand red vans in this state," Ken protested.

Detective Kwan opened an image file, tapped at keys, and then zoomed in on the grainy gray image of a van. Ken's heart soared, as he held his breath, hoping the means to track the abductors would fall neatly into their laps.

The detective grimaced, shook her head. "It's too blurred to make out the license plate."

Ken's heart sank.

Chapter 4
THE NOOSE TIGHTENS

Last chance—try to escape, or not?

Jessa's heart felt like it might explode inside her chest. The numbness in her limbs was wearing off, but they still tingled, and she wasn't sure how well her legs would function. She knew her captor would only need a microsecond to squeeze the trigger on that gun; the woman had nasty fast reflexes.

Jessa had never been much for math, but she was quite certain the odds of getting shot far outweighed her likelihood of getting away. On the other hand, she had zilch chance of escape so long as she was chained to the van, and this could be her last opportunity to take fate into her own hands. She remembered a saying from Mr. Chesterton's humanities class: "Fortune favors the brave." *Dear God, let that be true.*

Jessa held the restroom door open as she urged all her energies to focus. Every instant was about to count. No margin for error. She glanced down at her side and saw the barrel of the pistol inches away.

"Hey, Babe—" Dylan called from the van.

Bonnie turned back in his direction.

Now!

Jessa grabbed her captor's wrist with her left hand, snatched the gun barrel with her right. Then she threw herself toward the floor as she twisted her torso, hoping to break the woman's trigger finger. The woman screamed, and the gun clattered onto the floor. Jessa kicked it, then turned to run.

An angry scream filled her ears, and a foot hooked itself around her feet, tripping her. She fell, but she immediately struggled to her feet, only to be shoved backward. She struggled to refill her lungs.

The cold barrel of the pistol pushed hard against the side of Jessa's head. "Filthy little twit. You are so going to regret that," the woman hissed. "Now, you can get back in the van quietly, or shall I squeeze just a little bit?"

Slowly and painfully, Jessa pulled herself up and limped back to the van.

"Go ahead and pee on yourself," her tormentor said as she locked Jessa's handcuffs. "You broke my fingernails," she added, as if that were the worst thing that had ever happened to her.

The van started up again, this time with the woman driving.

Jessa glanced at Heather. The girl across from her was crying.

"Call our contact," Bonnie told Dylan. "I don't feel like stopping in Kingman. Tell him there had to be a change of plan. We'll make the deal in Barstow, at the Motel 6 on the east end of town."

"So, you're going with my idea?"

"Shut up and call."

Jessa had been in some bad situations before: dynamited in a cave on one case, poisoned on another case, and threatened by workers from a major corporation in a third CSC adventure. But she knew she had never faced such a formidable opponent. Bonnie didn't seem to make mistakes, and her reflexes were entirely unaffected by any sense of compassion or remorse.

Closing her eyes, Jessa thought of all the things she would miss: her mother, for one, despite all the years she'd spent angry at her mom, disgusted by her shortcomings. And things had changed—improved—so much in the past months. Her mother had quit smoking pot, and she'd apologized with tears for the ways she wronged her daughter in her childhood. Finally, after seventeen years, Jessa's mother was truly her friend. What an awful time to have to say goodbye.

Next, she pictured the pine-scented trails behind her house that lead up the side of the San Francisco Peaks, the endless contented hours she'd spent riding a horse or a bicycle along the winding mountain paths. She thought of her easel and acrylics and brushes, and the days she spent happily dabbing colors onto the canvas.

Happy memories of afternoons with Crime Scene Club entered her mind next. She thought of Lupe, bright and intense; Wire, exasperating genius that he was; and Maeve—how she would miss that crazy, inspired, nutcase. Even now, in this van from hell, if Maeve was here, Jessa knew she would find some way to make it all funny. If only Jessa could spend a few more minutes with her CSC friends before the end came, how wonderful that would be.

Jessa's mind moved now to the nights she'd spent singing with her old group, Red, White, and Blues. *Guess I'll never see that big music contract.*

Thinking of the band made Ken's face come to the foreground of her consciousness. Regret washed over her like waters bursting through a shattered dam. Yes, he could be a jerk. He had hurt her badly. And yet her happiest hours were the times they had shared. No one had ever touched her heart, no one had ever understood and cherished her the way Ken did.

He had begged her to come back. He had humbled himself, practically cried into his coffee cup at Café Paradiso, but she had been too proud to forgive him. If Ken could be in the van with her right now, even for an instant, she would tell him, just with a look of her eyes, that she was sorry. *I forgive you. I take it all back. I love you.*

She snapped back to her surroundings when the van hit a bump, jolting her tailbone and cuffed wrists. Her bladder was excruciatingly full now. She couldn't see her watch, cuffed behind her, but from the slant of the light coming through the van's windows, she guessed it was around five in the afternoon.

Nine more hours until. . .

Don't think of that. Pray for a miracle.

"We're doing what again?" Ken bit his lip, annoyed. *Time's running out for Jessa—and all we have is this awful blurred image.*

"It's basic application of two-dimensional calculus," Wire explained. "In other words, we utilize the real-valued functions of two real variables."

I know I've heard that in class, but I don't get it.

Ken tried to control his impatience as the geek attempted another explanation. "Okay, let's say that we have this video image coming across on a 650x500 pixel grade. We want to enlarge that to 1300x1000 pixels, in order to make out the plate on that van. But of course, enlarging just gives us bigger blocks in the image mosaic—no good. To sharpen the image as we enlarge, we need to use segmentation techniques, and we do that by giving every pixel an 'x' and 'y' coordinate. Got that?"

"Nope." Ken shook his head.

"Let it go, Wire," Detective Kwan sighed. "Long story short, you're using a set of calculations to improve the quality of the gas station surveillance images. Have you downloaded all the necessary applications into this desktop?"

"You got it, Ms. K. Just double-click where it says, 'apply' and—voila."

All three stared at the monitor as the policewoman tapped on her mouse. The van's tail end moved closer, tripled in size on the screen.

"Hey," Ken exclaimed, "I can make out the first letter now, that's an 'A.'"

"And the first number," Ms. Kwan added, "is definitely 'five.'"

"The others are hard to be sure of," Ken noted. "Wire, can we get better than this?"

"Afraid not. Even though it's been twenty years since Dr. Leonid Rudin developed this technique, there's still the limitation that statistical probabilities fail to distinguish—"

"All right, all right." Ken threw up his hands. "Ms. Kwan, do we have enough to—"

"That's our suspect's van," the detective said, her tone indicating an end to the technical discussion.

"So what do we do?"

"I'm calling for an alert, every point between Kingman and Barstow. We pull out all the stops—local law enforcement, media, the works. It's small towns all the way, and that will be an advantage finding them."

"We've been working on this forty-five minutes," Wire mused. "Assuming they continue west, they should be passing through Needles about now."

"Into California's jurisdiction," Ken said, bitterly. "Ms. Kwan, does that mean we're off the case?"

"Not if I can help it. I'll have my boss phone up California Highway Patrol and San Bernardino County PD, and see if they're willing to let us cooperate on this one. If they're game, I'm going to try and requisition a chopper. I want to be there when authorities apprehend that van."

Ken suddenly felt light-headed. "If they screw up the arrest, sometimes in kidnap cases . . . it happens that. . ." He couldn't finish the sentence.

"Dude, it'll be okay." Wire put his hand on Ken's shoulder. "These guys know what they're doing."

Detective Kwan nodded agreement as she picked up a phone.

For the next hour, Wire busied himself with probability programs, trying to guess where the most likely place of apprehension would be. Ken felt ready to punch something—or bang his head on the wall. He chose to pace up and down the hallway, instead.

It was almost six o'clock when Detective Kwan stuck her head into the hall. "All systems go. We can't be involved in the arrest—but we can be nearby to observe and then question. The other agencies involved recognize our obvious interest in Jessa's well-being."

"And the chopper?"

"Ready to take off. I'm headed there now."

"Detective Kwan, let me go with you. I have to be there, when—"

"I'm sorry, Ken. You know I can't involve you. All the cases we've been in and the liability issues that have come up—"

"Detective Kwan, please."

The policewoman bit her lip.

"Ms. Kwan, it's Jessa in that van." Ken's voice cracked.

She sighed and nodded. "But you stay out of the action—just observe, no matter what happens. I have your word?"

"Absolutely."

"All right, let's get in the air."

They said goodbye to Wire, who had no interest in flying. As they left the building, Ken asked Detective Kwan, "Where exactly are we going?"

"Wire did some more probability analysis of the situation. He calculated in some new information on their route before Albuquerque and their path heading west. He's guessing they'll stop in Barstow."

"How sure is that?"

"He says there's an 80 percent probability. We've asked the Barstow PD to notify gas stations, restaurants, motels, and bars—everyone who might spot that van."

"Sounds good," Ken agreed.

A few minutes later, Ken double-checked his seat belt as the noise and vibration increased, indicating the helicopter was about to mount into the air.

Seated next to him behind the pilot, Detective Kwan asked, "Have you ridden in a helicopter before?"

He nodded. "With my dad." But this time, he felt more nervous. It wasn't so much concern about the flight, as what he might have to deal with when the helicopter landed.

"Everyone ready?" the pilot asked through the intercom.

Ms. Kwan gave him a thumb up, the pilot flipped a couple of switches, and the chopper began its ascent. As soon as it had reached cruising altitude, the aircraft moved rapidly over Interstate 40, heading west. "We're going about two hundred knots per hour—fast as she'll move," the pilot told his passengers.

"That's good," Detective Kwan said.

The sun was setting ahead of them, bathing the mountains and forests below in hues of orange, brandy red, and chocolate brown. Ken glanced at his watch. Almost seven at night now, and Jessa had vanished sometime around noon. *Please, let her be okay.*

After fifty minutes in the air, the pilot told them, "Radio message coming in, I'll send it to you."

A voice crackled, "Detective Kwan?"

"Roger."

"This is Captain Caleb Smith with the Barstow Police Department. We just now received a tip that a red van with a couple driving, along with a car full of young people—apparently a sales crew, from their conversation—has checked into the Motel Six just east of town. The license numbers do not match your vehicle, but the couple's description sounds like the two folks you're looking for."

"Did they check in with a card?"

"Negative. Used cash. Do you want us to move in?"

"Affirmative, as soon as you can. Remember, they're keeping at least one, maybe two young women hostage."

"Roger that."

Detective Kwan glanced over at Ken, then added, "Captain Smith?"

"Yes, Detective?"

"We're coming into town now. I'm seeing some hotels and restaurants on the outskirts. Any chance we could land quickly and ride along with your team when they close in?"

There was a brief pause; then, "Do you see that big empty field to the north, just above a row of tract homes?"

"I see it."

"If your pilot agrees, you can put down there. We've got two units coming along the road that borders that field. We can pick you up in a few minutes."

"Can do," the pilot affirmed. "Bringing her down now."

Ken was ready to leap out as soon as the helicopter settled, kicking up a whirlwind of sand and dust. "Wait," Detective Kwan reminded him. "We'll get out as soon as the rotors stop."

She thanked the pilot, and a minute later, the two scurried out toward the road. They could see two black-and-white SUVs, their lights flashing but sirens off, racing along the street toward them. They stopped, and Ms. Kwan and Ken were ushered into the back of the rear car. They quickly exchanged introductions.

"We'll be at the motel in a couple of minutes," the officer at the wheel explained. "A third unit is meeting us there."

Ken's heart was pounding. What if these officers messed up the arrest? Was Jessa injured? Was she even alive?

Chapter 5
UNAUTHORIZED PURSUIT

As the police vehicles neared the motel, they shut off their sirens. The two SUVs pulled into an access road to the rear of the parking lot, away from the motel office. A squad car joined them, and the officers leapt out.

The policeman driving the second SUV turned to his passengers. "Detective Kwan, you're free to follow us—but only as an observer."

"Of course."

"Young man, you have to stay here."

"But, I—"

"No buts. This is close as you go."

Officers jumped out of the vehicles and sprinted toward the other end of the motel complex. Ms. Kwan squeezed Ken's hand and stepped out to follow them. And then the driver pressed a button on his remote key chain and locked Ken into the rear of the vehicle.

I don't believe it! He knew CSC had gotten into all sorts of trouble over the past year, and that the Barstow PD was just being cautious. Still, he chafed inwardly.

His palms were moist. He saw the officers run down the parking lot, then up a flight of stairs and out of his sight. What was going on up there? Was Jessa in the room? Was she hurt?

As Ken fretted, imprisoned in the back of the truck, he saw a door open from a nearby, ground-level room. Two figures emerged.

One was Jessa. Her mouth was gagged with duct tape, and her hands were cuffed behind her.

Next to Jessa was a woman dressed in a business suit. She held a gun to Jessa's ribs. The woman hurried Jessa around the back corner of the building.

Cursing inwardly, Ken looked back at the other end of the motel, where the officers and Detective Kwan had disappeared. There was no sight of them; apparently they were unaware of Jessa's situation. He pulled out his cell phone, speed-dialed for Ms. Kwan.

No answer. They might have apprehended half the crew—but Jessa and her captor were getting away. Ken pulled at the door handle. Of course, nothing happened. He pounded his fist on the window.

Crazy with frustration, Ken acted without thinking. He leaned back in the seat, drew his booted legs back, and kicked with all his might at the window. At the first kick, nothing happened. With a second kick, it cracked into a spider-web pattern. On the third effort, the glass shattered outward. He grabbed a clipboard that had been left on the seat beside him and hurriedly knocked away the jagged shards that protruded from

the bottom of the window; then he backed out through the opening, landing boots first on the glass-strewn parking lot.

He dashed around the side of the hotel, and saw Jessa's captor get into a red van that had been partially concealed behind an eighteen-wheeler on the outskirts of the lot. He assumed Jessa was already inside. The vehicle's motor started.

He had to get pursuit on that van—not a second to waste. If he ran down the length of the building and alerted the others, he was afraid it would take a long time—too long—to explain what happened. They'd focus on how he got out of the SUV and perhaps ignore the real urgency of the situation because he'd defied their authority.

He ran back toward the vehicle he'd arrived in and noted the other black-and-white SUV parked next to it. He tried the door.

It opened. The keys were in the ignition.

Ken jumped into the driver's seat and fired up the motor. As he did so, he saw the red van out of the corner of his eye, pulling rapidly out of the parking lot. He jammed the SUV into gear and pulled out after the van. The van accelerated rapidly, and Ken did the same.

For several minutes, the two vehicles sped up, driving on a straight stretch of road headed north out of town. The intercom crackled. "This is Captain Smith to Unit 9. Who's driving? And where are you going?"

Man, that was fast. Ken hesitated, then replied. "This is Unit 9. Red van has escaped with hostage, back along the same route we came in on. Driver is armed. Over."

The responding voice sounded livid. "Are you that kid that came out from Arizona? Pull over right now, son, or I swear when this is over we'll—"

Ken decided to ignore him.

The red van was still speeding up, and he pressed the throttle to stay with it. He glanced at the dash: they were going ninety-five. Ken wasn't used to speeds like this, and his stomach twisted as he thought how unstable that big van ahead would be at this pace.

Sweat dripped off his forehead and he wiped it away from his eyes. His mind racing with adrenaline, he hadn't really thought through a course of action. Now, for the first time in several minutes, his head cleared long enough to think.

He was in pursuit, but had no way to make the other driver pull over and stop. Clearly, this kidnapper was desperate yet resourceful. She knew she was being followed and had no intention of slowing down. Besides that, the kidnapper was armed. Ken's eyes darted around the cab. He had no weapon; the driver had grabbed the shotgun from its rack. Nor did he have any idea what he would do if the van should stop. Meanwhile, the woman held Jessa's life at gunpoint. Ken knew he was out on a limb—and he had the feeling it was about to break.

"We're being followed."

Jessa did not care for the tone in her captor's voice. Not that it mattered what she thought; she couldn't say or do a thing. The tape was still over her mouth, and Jessa's cuffed hands were again chained to the side of the vehicle.

"You've been nothing but trouble from the moment I saw you," the woman snarled over her shoulder.

As if this whole thing was my idea.

Judging from the vibration and sound of the motor, they were going incredibly fast. *Who's following us? The police?*

They'd been sitting in the hotel room—her kidnapper had been watching *Doctor Phil*, of all things—and commenting about the people on the show and how stupid they were. *Wish someone would give you mental health advice, Jessa was thinking. You need to get in touch with your inner psychopath.*

Then Bonnie had glanced out the window, muttered, "Cops," and pulled her gun out of a drawer. She jerked Jessa to her feet and pointed toward the door. "Move it. We're outta here."

Jessa wondered where Heather was. She hoped the other girl was all right, maybe even freed in the raid.

The van braked and swerved, interrupting Jessa's thoughts. Her cuffs tore into her wrists as she slammed against the side of the vehicle. *A three-quarter-ton van isn't exactly a sports car, but that doesn't stop this crazy lady from driving like it is.*

Bonnie let out a yelp. Jessa was again slammed against the side of the vehicle, and then momentum lifted her for an instant off of the floor. The van shot downward, and through the windshield, she caught a view of a long steep slope dead ahead.

Then the world spun around and around again. Jessa grabbed the eyelet on the van's side, so the chain wouldn't snap her wrist as she flew back and forth like a rag doll.

The vehicle came to an abrupt stop.

Jessa groaned, her mouth still gagged. She was sore and scraped in a half-dozen places. The van rested partially on its side. Through the shattered windshield ahead of her, Jessa looked along a rocky hillside. They had apparently flown off the road and rolled down the side of a ravine.

What about her captor? Had she been injured in the crash? The woman was not moving.

Then, Jessa caught a whiff of smoke.

Oh, oh. Yellow and orange flashes burst from the front of the vehicle. Jessa looked at her black-and-blue-and-bloody wrists, then pulled her aching arms against the chain. It still held.

"Oomph. Bad landing."

Guess Bonnie survived the crash.

The woman turned, looked back at Jessa, then glanced around for her gun. Jessa spied a metal barrel protruding from under the passenger's seat. She glanced away, hoping Bonnie wouldn't see it.

"Guess the fire will have to take care of you, girly," Bonnie was saying. "I can't stick around." She heaved against her door—which now pointed more upward than sideways—and pulled herself up and out of the van.

More smoke and flames billowed from the front of the van, and Jessa realized that eventually, the gas tank would explode. Her wheeled prison cell would turn into a funeral pyre.

She rolled onto her back and propped her feet against the side of the van. Then she saw something that shot a faint ray of hope into her heart. The eyelet, welded to the vehicle's side, was half broken-off.

Every muscle ached as she kicked both feet at once. The eyelet moved, just a tiny bit. Or was it her imagination?

She kicked again. Pain shot through her cuffed wrists, her scraped bottom, her jarred neck. But the metal coupling did move, this time she was sure.

Crack! The eyelet snapped clear of the wall, landing Jessa hard on the opposite side of the van. She scooted on her bottom to the rear door of the vehicle, fumbling at the latch with her hands still cuffed behind her back.

Locked or jammed, the door wouldn't budge. Meanwhile, the smoke inside the van was thickening—and Jessa was beginning to panic. She couldn't catch a breath. But the only way out lay through the front doors, where the smoke was worst.

She inhaled as deeply as her nose would allow, then stumbled forward. A quick glance at the passenger's door showed her it was jammed up against a boulder: no way out there.

With her hands fastened, she had to strain to reach upward to the driver's side door. She pushed herself skyward, feet against the passenger's seat and bottom on the driver's seat, pushing with aching shoulders to reach the door handle behind her back. Finally, her fingers felt the door latch. She pulled it, then shoved her shoulders back against the door.

It lifted. Jessa bent her knees, walked her feet over the seats—and pushed her body out of the van, onto the dirt of the slope.

Her nostrils opened wider, took in sweet breaths of fresh air. Glancing behind her, she saw that the crumpled red van was mounted precariously on the side of a rocky slope, the side of a ravine that extended downward more than a hundred feet into an immense quarry.

A blast of heat against her legs made her realize the fire was spreading. *Gotta crawl up and away before the gas tank goes*. She arched her back and pushed with her legs, trying to inch her pain-wracked body away from the van. Loose rock gave way beneath her, offering her no traction. *I have to get some distance—or I'm toast*, she thought grimly. She squirmed, tried to move higher, fighting the panic that threatened to overwhelm her.

"Jessa!"

It was the sweetest sound she'd ever heard. "Jessa, hold on, Babe. I'm almost there. I'll pull you up." She tilted her head and saw Ken scrambling down the side of the hill.

Is he real or am I dreaming?

His warm hands under her arms convinced her of his reality. He pulled both of them up and away from the burning vehicle. Jessa helped push them upward with her feet, but for every foot gained, a small pile of rock and dirt slid out from beneath them.

Ken gave a panicked shout. "Whoa—rock slide!"

The rubble beneath them gave way.

Ken shoved Jessa into on a small bush. He tried to grab the same plant, but his hand missed. Eyes wide, Jessa watched Ken slide down onto the van in a cloud of rubble. The van tilted beneath his weight.

And then, slowly but inexorably, the vehicle lurched forward and came free of the outcropping that had pinned it to the side of the slope. Jessa closed her eyes as the shattered, burning vehicle, with Ken atop it, slid down the hillside.

Her eyes were still shut, moments later, when she heard it explode.

Chapter 6
BROKEN

Ken wasn't sure how long he'd been lost in a delirium of painkillers. People in white coats came and went. He recognized faces, concerned voices: his dad, his mom, Jessa, Detective Kwan.

Finally, his head cleared enough for him to take stock of his surroundings and condition. A nurse told him he was in Barstow Community Hospital, and that he'd been there four days. His left hand, completely encased in a big cast, was shattered in more than a dozen places. He couldn't see out of his right eye—because it had been damaged. The nurse was reluctant to give details.

"I'll ask Dr. Chen to see you. He'll be able to tell you more."

Dr. Chen's voice was kind, but his words were anything but comforting. "Your hand has numerous breaks and fractures. We had to cut some muscles to set it."

"Will it recover fully?"

"No, I'm afraid not."

"Will I be able to use it at all?"

"Perhaps, for some simple things—holding an object against your other hand, for example. But not for fine work."

"So I'm crippled."

"You'll be impaired with that hand, but people are able to do many things without—"

"What about my eye?" Ken interrupted.

The doctor hesitated and seemed reluctant to answer.

"That bad, huh?"

"A chunk of metal flew into your eye from the explosion."

"Explosion?"

"You don't remember?"

Ken shook his head. "I remember flying to Barstow, and getting in a police car, not much after that." His thoughts cleared. "I know Jessa has been here. I remember seeing her face. Is she all right?"

"She's pretty upset, but physically, she's fine."

Ken smiled—or tried to; the side of his face hurt. "So, you were explaining, my eye—?"

"You've lost all vision in your right eye. Part of your cheek was cut as well."

"Cut?"

"Actually, sliced off by a fragment of the explosion. We'll do plastic surgery, after it heals. And you'll have a false eye."

"I'm a cripple and I'm scarred."

"You're a young man with a 90 percent healthy body. You'll do fine—but it will take some getting used to. I'm sorry to have to be the one to tell you." Dr. Chen glanced behind him at the door. "There's a young woman here who's been waiting to see you. I'll check back in a couple of hours."

He left the room as Jessa came and sat beside the bed. She took Ken's good hand in hers. The scent of Jessa's patchouli perfume and the sight of her blue eyes calmed him and gave him a new sense of strength.

"Hey," she said.

"Hey."

"You've been out of it."

"Four days, they tell me. I remember you, Mom, Dad, Ms. Kwan. . . . Not much else."

"Lupe, Wire, and Maeve have all been here, too. They girls just got back from Mexico. They're at a motel down the road. I phoned and told them you're awake now. They'll be here soon."

"Did Maeve and Lupe have a good time on their trip?"

"They're all tan. Maeve did something scandalous—I'll let her tell the story. Do you remember Mr. Peshlaki visiting you?"

Ken shook his head.

"He sprinkled yellow stuff over you, chanted for half a day."

"Corn pollen. He did a healing ceremony."

"I heard your dad say something about spending his whole year's bonus for that."

Ken tried smiling, slowly. He didn't want to think about what the doctor had told him, so he focused instead on Jessa's face, her words. "Medicine men are just like white doctors—they have to live somehow. But what's your story? I mean, I came to your house and you were gone, and—I'm missing your side of this case."

"Sure you're up for this?"

"I am." He gave her a crooked grin, not wanting her to see how scared he was. "But if it's too hard to remember. . . ?"

"No. I have to work through it . And if I can't tell you, who can I tell?" So Jessa told him how she met Heather at the door, how Dylan and Bonnie captured her, and how she'd been held at the hotel until the police raid. She ended with the van crash.

"What happened after I fell?"

"I . . . I wasn't actually looking. I closed my eyes, the van exploded and . . . I thought you were dead. . . but you were lying beside it, maybe fifteen feet away. You must have been thrown clear before it went off."

"How long did you have to wait for help?"

"Only a few minutes. The police were there just after you arrived, and medics right behind them."

"What happened to the woman—Bonnie?"

"The police mounted a manhunt. They found her hiding in the brush next morning. She's in jail, along with her husband. The rest of the sales crew have gone home. They were just pawns in the operation."

"What about Heather, the girl who started all this?"

"She's with her mom in Chicago. We've talked a few times over the computer. She might come out and stay with me this summer. I want her to meet the other CSC kids."

Ken sighed. "Speaking of CSC, this whole incident is probably the nail in the coffin for the club—pardon the expression."

Jessa nodded. "It was gonna be shut down anyway. Crazy idea to start with. But we had an amazing time."

"We did, for sure."

"There's more about the case," Jessa offered. "Want to hear it?"

"Of course."

"Even after the arrest, things were challenging for the authorities. The drugs were gone from the van. There were traces left, but you couldn't tell how much Bonnie and Dylan had sold. There were record books in the van, but those were coded. The local detectives couldn't make head nor tail of them. The police interrogated Dylan and Bonnie, but neither of them would admit a thing. Captain Smith and Ms. Kwan did the good-cop–bad-cop gig, but they wouldn't say a peep." She shook her head. "So when they came out to see you, Ms. K was telling the CSC about all these problems, and Wire says, 'Can I see the coded book?'"

"Let me guess, he cracked it."

"Yep. Fired up his laptop, and said it was a simple matter of algorithms."

Ken groaned. "Those are on my final exam. It's a way to take a set and go through a process, producing a whole other set of outcomes. Gives me a headache."

"Well, I don't think you'll have to take that final exam for a while. If you're in the hospital for a week,

I'm guessing they'll give you an extension."

"So Wire cracked the code?"

"Yup. Came up with a detailed list of drugs picked up and dropped off, along with contacts."

"Sweet."

"That's not all. Bonnie and Dylan still wouldn't confess—even when Ms. K showed them the decoded entries. So Wire got special permission to sit down with them in the interrogation room. He wrote formulas on a whiteboard—something he calls 'loss equations.' Explained how mathematically, Bonnie had nothing to lose from keeping her mouth shut, given her past legal history and everything she'd done."

"That sounds like a stupid thing to tell her."

"She wasn't going to talk anyway. But then Wire went on and showed Dylan how much the odds were against him if he kept quiet, and how much better off he'd be if he squealed on his wife."

"No, you're kidding. . ."

Jessa shook her head. "As soon as they were separated from each other, he spilled the beans all over."

Ken grinned, winced, tried not to think about his face. "So this whole case was pretty much solved by the numbers."

"If it weren't for Wire's calculations, I'd be dead by now." Jessa shuddered.

"Mmm."

"What are you thinking?"

"I've always wanted to be a cop. Figured I'd be like my Dad—a good officer, out on the streets. But frankly, with one eye and only one usable hand. . ."

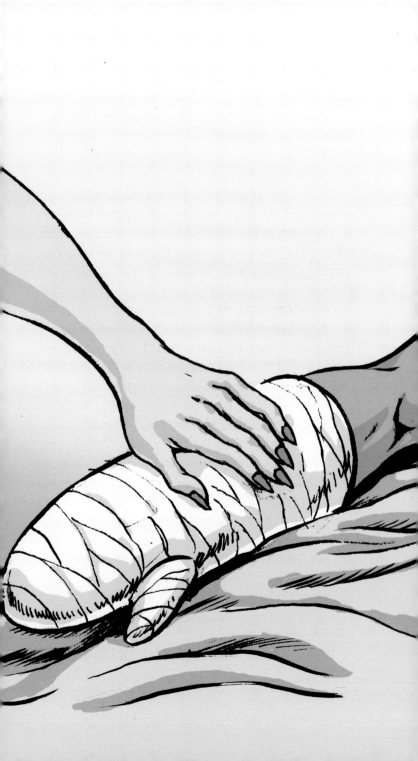

"There's a million other things you can do," Jessa said quickly.

"Like lab work. We need good patrol men—but we need good analysts, too."

"Sounds like you better keep working on those forensics courses."

"Yep. Even math." Ken leaned back, sighed. He was scared, hurting, but none of it seemed to matter as much as the fact that he and Jessa were together, talking the way they used to. He knew he could say anything, and she'd understand. "I'm never going to look the same again."

"They'll do surgery."

"Yeah, but that fake eye will always seem weird. This hand won't be any better than a prosthetic. Who's going to want a broken ex-jock?"

Jessa took her free hand and put it on his cast. "I think these are the loveliest fingers in the world."

"They're gonna be all bent, ugly."

"Shh." She put a finger to his lips. "They're perfect." She moved her hand to his cheek, running a gentle finger over the bandages. "And this is the loveliest face I've ever seen."

He winced and muttered, "A glass ball in my eye socket, a scarred cheek. . ." He looked at her, searching her face for any sign she was repulsed.

She leaned closer to him. "It's the face I want to look at for the rest of my life."

Ken felt his fears ease. Even the pain loosed its hold on him.

If he and Jessa were together, he had all he really needed.

FORENSIC NOTES

CRIME SCENE CLUB, CASE #11

CHAPTER 1

Evidence List

Vocab Words

contemplated
crestfallen
peers
nonconformity
furtively
waif
hyperventilating
stiletto
assent

Deciphering the Evidence

Jessa *contemplates*, or looks carefully and thoughtfully at, the young woman who is selling magazine subscriptions.

The girl appears *crestfallen* at Jessa's response to the magazine selection she offers. She is disappointed that Jessa does not seem to be interested in any of the choices she suggests.

Jessa's friend Maeve has an attitude that causes her *peers* to cower in her presence. Peers are people of the same age group or standing.

Jessa notices that Heather has the same conforming-to-*nonconformity* style that Maeve has. Nonconformity means refusal to go along with the crowd.

When Jessa invites the girl in, Heather looks *furtively* to both sides. Furtively means slyly or secretively; she doesn't want Jessa to see that she's unsure about entering the house.

Jessa suspects that this door-to-door *waif* is lugging a heavy burden. A waif is a stray person or animal.

As she nears the end of her story, Heather starts *hyperventilating* or breathing very rapidly and deeply.

After Jessa hits the concrete of the patio, she looks up to see a *stiletto* heel on her throat. Stiletto heels are long, thin, pointed, and sharp.

When Bonnie commands Dylan to pull the van back, he mutters *assent*, or agreement.

The World of Forensics

Our English word "forensic" comes from the Latin word *forensis*, which means "forum"—the public area where in the days of ancient Rome a person charged with a crime presented his case. Both the person accused of the crime and the accuser would give speeches presenting their sides of the story. The person with the best forensic skills usually won the case.

In the modern world, "forensics" has come to mean the various procedures, many of them scientific in nature, used to answer questions of interest to the legal system—usually, to solve a crime. Detective Kwan and the members of the CSC use many of these procedures in their cases. In this case, their eleventh, the procedures involved with forensic mathematics will prove to be particularly useful to them.

Forensic Math Procedures

Hypothesis Testing

Hypothesis testing uses statistics to test if a hypothesis is valid. A hypothesis is an educated guess or explanation based on an observation. Hypotheses are part of the scientific method of study, which includes a question, research and observation, forming a hypothesis, testing the hypothesis, analyzing the results, and retesting as necessary.

Hypothesis testing is normally done in four steps:

1. Write a null hypothesis, which is a statement that is created only to be disproved.

2. Choose an observed test statistic that can be used to test the truth of the null hypothesis.

3. Figure out the p-value, which is the probability that the test statistic is at least as significant as the one observed would be, assuming that the null hypothesis were true. In statistics, the smaller the p-value, the stronger the evidence against the null hypothesis (meaning the

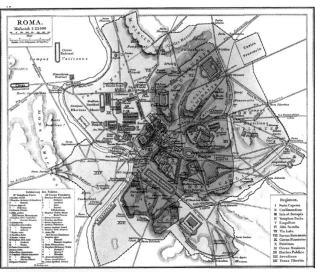

1.1 The forum, from which we get the modern word forensics, was the center of ancient Rome.

stronger the evidence is for the hypothesis).

4. Compare the p-value to a number called an alpha value. If p<=alpha, the observed effect is statistically significant, the null hypothesis is false, and the hypothesis is valid.

Algorithms

An algorithm is a sequence of ordered steps that can be used to solve a problem. There is usually also a requirement that the operation has a stopping point. Algorithms are typically used to solve complex problems, such as mathematical formulas or instructions given by a computer program.

Neural Networks?

An artificial neural network, which is often just called a "neural network," is a mathematical model based on the networks of neurons in brains and nervous systems of living biological organisms. In a biological neural network, thousands of neurons, or nerve cells, form an interconnected web. When one neuron gets a message at its dendrites, the message travels through the axon of the neuron and jumps from the terminal buttons, across a gap (called a synapse) to the next neuron. In an

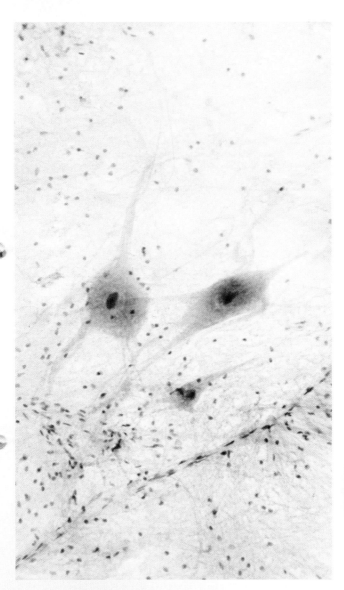

1.2 Artificial neural networks are modeled after the structure and function of biological nerve cells, like the ones shown here.

1.3 Bayesian probability analysis uses past events to "guess" the likelihood of future events. It is often applied in spam e-mail filtering, computer medical diagnosis and game-playing.

artificial neural network, simple nodes (called "neurons," "neurodes," "processing elements" [PEs], or "units") are connected together to form the network.

Like a nervous system, an artificial neural network changes its behavior depending on the information that is flowing through it. In an artificial network, information is comes from a computer or from another external source that enters algorithms to tell the network what to do.

Neural networks can be used as statistical modeling tools or to find patterns in data. They are especially useful in extremely complex situations where it would take too long to figure the pattern out by hand.

Some of the real-life applications include: vehicle-control, game-playing and decision making, medical diagnosis, face identification, and e-mail spam filtering.

Bayesian Analysis

Bayesian analysis is a statistical guess that tries to estimate the probability of future events based on the knowledge of prior events.

Bayesian techniques have recently been used to filter spam e-mail, by using a reference set of e-mails to define spam. The filter then uses the reference to decide whether new incoming messages are spam or good e-mail. New e-mail messages act as new information. If the user identifies mistakes in the definitions of spam and good e-mail, this new information overwrites the original reference definition in the hope that future filtering is more accurate.

What Is Hapkido?

Hapkido is the Korean art of self-defense. While other types of martial arts use force against force, Hapkido uses the attacker's power against himself through techniques such as diversion. Size and strength are not important factors because practitioners of Hapkido use pressure on skeletal joints and pressure points to help suppress their attacker. These strategies are in keeping with the Hapkido philosophy of discipline and avoidance of violence.

Why Do Kool-Aid and Cyanide Go Together?

When Heather describes her managers and crew, Jessa suggests that Heather should be careful or she might find herself drinking Kool-Aid and cyanide. Jessa thinks Heather may be dealing with a cult. Jessa is using the term in its modern sense to refer to social groups defined by a set of beliefs or practices that fall outside mainstream society. However, in its earliest usage the word cult originally referred to religious worship and rituals, especially as practiced in temples, shrines, and churches. The word comes from the Latin cultus, which means "to care for or cultivate," and literally referred to the necessity to care for a shrine and the god for which the shrine was built.

Today, the word cult still implies a "worship" of something, but the power being worshipped varies from a traditional spirit to a B horror flick. However, in many cases cults are still driven by religious or spiritual purposes. At other times, money or power is the driving force behind the formation of a cult. The crew that Heather works for seems to be focused mostly on controlling its employees and making money.

The other characteristic typical of cults is the existence of a single, powerful person who guides or controls the followers within the cult. Jessa recognizes such a person in Heather's description of Bonnie. Leaders of cults are people who can make others follow them. Heather says Bonnie seemed like the type of woman she wanted to be, so it was easy to admire her and want to please her. This charisma and ability to gain admirers is how cult leaders thrive. Cult leaders also keep control of their followers through fear. Heather is too afraid of the consequences to try and leave so she stays with her crew despite terrible circumstances. In some cults, people follow their leaders even to death.

The Jonestown Massacre

The group known as the People's Temple was founded in Indiana in 1955 by the Reverend James Warren Jones, more commonly called simply Jim Jones. Jones became a Christian minister in order to expose his socialist ideals to a wider populace. The People's Temple began as a mission that welcomed the sick and homeless of any race. As a result, Jones gained a huge following. The group moved to California and then to Jonestown, Guyana, in 1977 where they started the "Peoples Temple Agricultural Project."

It was in Jonestown that tragedy struck. The project was supposed to be an ideal example of an egalitarian community where everyone lived off the land in harmony. However, it became a prison instead. People were held there against their will and were tortured or killed

killed if they complained or tried to escape. Finally, on November 18, 1978, Jones ordered all of his followers to drink punch poisoned with cyanide. Over 900 people died as a part of this mass murder-suicide that Jones saw as necessary for translation, his belief that if they all died together they would travel together to another planet for a life in paradise. Jessa's comment about Kool-Aid and cyanide is in reference to the Jonestown massacre; there is even a popular saying: "Don't drink the Kool-Aid," that warns not to blindly follow authority.

CHAPTER 2

Evidence List

Vocab Words

befuddled
muse
fetish
skeptical
disharmony
detachment
subdued
preliminary
accomplice
assailant
abduction
canvassed
APB

Deciphering the Evidence

Ken is *befuddled* or confused by many of his first-year lectures at Northern Arizona University.

As he sits daydreaming in his dorm room, Ken realizes that Jessa had been many things to him, including his *muse*. A muse is an inspiring being.

When he reaches Jessa's house, Ken rubs the *fetish* around his neck for good luck. A fetish is an object thought to have magical powers.

The Navajo elders believed that a botched relationship was the result of human *disharmony* or conflict.

Moments after Ken calls Detective Kwan, she appears at Jessa's house with a *detachment*—or specialized unit—of officers.

When Ken says quietly that it looks like there has been a struggle, Detective Kwan responds in an equally *subdued* tone. Subdued means soft or hushed.

Detective Kwan offers Ken the *preliminary* observation that someone entered Jessa's house through the unlocked screen door. Preliminary means occurring early on or at the beginning.

Detective Kwan further speculates that the intruder or an *accomplice* pulled their vehicle onto the back lawn. An accomplice is someone who helps another person commit a crime.

Ken finishes Detective Kwan's thought, saying that the assailant drove away with Jessa. An *assailant* is an attacker.

Detective Kwan tells Ken that they have to treat the incident as an *abduction*, or kidnapping.

An officer reports back to Detective Kwan that he has *canvassed* all the houses on Jessa's street. This means he has gone through the area to get information from people.

Detective Kwan radios in an *APB* describing the magazine salesgirl and the van. An APB is an all points bulletin, or a bulletin to be shared with other law enforcement personnel telling them to be on the lookout for a suspect or vehicle that may be involved in a crime.

Forensic Procedures Used in CSC Case #11

Gathering Clues from Witnesses

Despite a general trend toward heavily scientific forensic investigations, witnesses still provide the backbone of many cases. The first step in any crime scene investigation is always to gather as many witnesses as possible, in order to question them for information. Especially early on, witness testimony can have a dramatic effect on the course of an investigation, particularly in how police look into suspects. What an innocent bystander may have seen and how well he or she remembers it may mean the difference between catching a suspect and letting a criminal roam free.

2.1 Police gather information from a witness at a crime scene. Witnesses are important for identifying suspects early in the case, as well as in the courtroom.

Witness testimony in court is also vitally important in a criminal investigation. The problem with witnesses is that often their stories can be contested, because they may not have a perfect memory of the crime. This can leave room for doubt about their version of events. Especially in the modern era, where DNA evidence is all but a sure thing, witness testimony is important, because it can be helpful if accurate, and hurtful if untrue or faulty.

Piecing Together Information

As clues from the crime scene, witness inquiries, and further investigation begin to take shape, police must make connections between these different aspects of a case. The job of investigators is to make sense of various stories from witnesses and suspects, all while considering the evidence. Forensics is almost entirely based on the collection of information. This information—these clues—must be viewed together and then a narrative of what happened at a crime scene, or where a criminal went after committing a crime, must be made. This narrative serves as the basis for criminal investigation.

CHAPTER 3

Evidence List

Vocab Words

lethal
nonchalantly
intuited
deviations
apogee
transition
extrinsic motivation

Deciphering the Evidence

Jessa had known from the start that she
and Heather were in *lethal*—or deadly—
peril.

From the back of the van, Jessa can tell
that Bonnie is working *nonchalantly* on
a crossword puzzle while Dylan drives.
Bonnie seems totally unconcerned about
the fact that they have just kidnapped two
young women.

In the short time that she has known
Bonnie, Jessa has *intuited*—or sensed by
intuition—a lot about the woman.

Bonnie tells Dylan that any *deviations*—or
changes—from their previous plans will
look suspicious.

Detective Kwan tells Ken that an *apogee* has been established for traveling along Interstate 40, from Albuquerque to Holbrook to Flagstaff, taking a day for each *transition*. Apogee in this instance means the farthest point a vehicle can travel along that route every day. Transition means a passage or change from one point to another.

Wire speculates that the kidnappers have some *extrinsic motivation* for the course they're on. He means that there is an outside or external purpose or reason for what they are doing.

Forensic Techniques Used in CSC Case #11

Establishing an Operations Command Center

The first step of any investigation is establishing an operations command center. Investigations are based almost entirely on information, and this information must be managed effectively if investigations are to succeed. The operations command center provides the management of resources and information needed to organize an investigation. The command center takes in all the information of an investigation, and then gives out orders. It is the core of any investigation.

Checking Credit Card Use

More than ever, credit cards are everywhere, and almost everyone has one. These cards allow for electronic transfer of money, and have made life easier for many people. Investigators have profited from the rise of credit cards as well, using them to track down criminals and put them behind bars. Due to the electronic nature of credit cards, transactions and payments are all

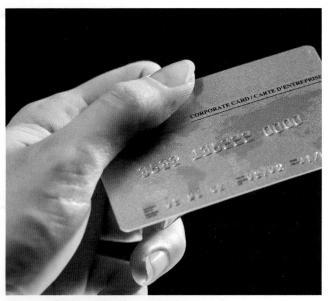

3.1 Credit cards are a quick and convenient way to buy—just swipe now and pay later. They have also become a source of theft. Computer savvy criminals can collect information stored in the strip, and use it to access the owner's account and possibly even their identity.

recorded. This information can be accessed by the cardholder or the credit card company, but it can also be used by the police to track the whereabouts, activities, and purchases of wanted criminals. By working with credit card companies during an investigation, police can examine credit card records for clues about the location of suspects, all by looking at what they buy and where they buy it.

Forensic Math Techniques

Probability Analysis

This technique is a process for analyzing possible future events by considering possible alternative outcomes or scenarios. The purpose of this analysis is to help decision-makers assess situations by allowing more complete consideration of outcomes and their implications. It's a technique that's used in many fields besides forensics.

For example, in economics and finance, a financial institution (such as a bank) might attempt to forecast several possible scenarios for the economy (for example, rapid growth, moderate growth, or slow growth) and it might also attempt to forecast financial market returns for each of these possible scenarios. It might then determine sub-sets of each of the possibilities—and then analyze these still further by assigning probabilities to the

3.2 Economists at the New York Stock Exchange use probability analysis to predict changes in the economy. Traders decide which stocks to buy or sell based on these predictions.

scenarios (and additional sub-sets if any). Then financial institution will be able to decide how spread its assets between various investments. Similarly, in politics, probability analysis involves determining the possible alternative paths of a social or political environment and possible diplomatic and war risks. For example, in the recent Iraq War, the Pentagon would have listed the possibilities that might arise in the war situation and positioned troops accordingly.

This same techniques can be applied to crime-solving, which is what Wire does. By listing all possible scenarios that the criminals might choose to act out, forensic analysts can determine which are the most likely, allowing police to respond accordingly.

Existent Pattern

When analyzing probability, forensic mathematicians look for an already existent pattern. In other words, if a criminal has behaved in a certain way in the past under certain conditions, the probability is higher that he will behave that way again in the same circumstance than that he won't.

Apogee

The apogee is the most distant point likely to be reached. Wire is able to determine this

3.3 Probability analysis is also important in wartime, when deciding where to position troops. United States troops are positioned in Iraq based on analysis by the Pentagon to determine where the troops are most needed.

by looking at the existent pattern of how far the suspects are traveling each day and how fast.

Equation for Probability

Forensic mathematicians use a number of equations for determining probability. Here are some examples:

The probability that you will draw an ace when pulling a card at random from a shuffled deck of cards equals the total number of cards in a deck divided by the number of aces in a deck. This means that

Probability = 54/4 = 13.5

The probability that if you flip a coin it will come up heads twice in a row is determined by multiply the probability that you will get heads once (1/2) twice or

Probability = 1/2 x 1/2 = 1/4

Who Was Thomas Bayes?

Thomas Bayes was an eighteenth-century mathematician and Presbyterian minister known for his theorem of probability, called Baye's Theorem. Baye's Theorem helps to explain how the probability that something is true is affected by the availability of new information. A good example of Baye's Theorem in action is a doctor who examines the patient on a number of occasions and, as a result, becomes progressively more certain of his or her diagnosis based on the changing a priori knowledge of the patient. The probability of making a correct diagnosis is increased by the physician's increasing experience with the patient.

3.4 Thomas Bayes

CHAPTER 4

Evidence List

Vocab Words

excruciatingly
pixel grade
mosaic
requisition
apprehension
liability
knots
rotors

Deciphering the Evidence

After being denied the chance to visit the restroom, Jessa's bladder is *excruciatingly*—or painfully—full.

Wire uses an example of a video image with a *pixel grade* of 650 x 500 to explain two-dimensional calculus to Ken. Pixel grade refers to the quality of an image based on the number of pixels—dots of light or color—it contains.

Wire explains to Ken that enlarging the video image of the license plate only makes the blocks in the image *mosaic* bigger, it doesn't sharpen the picture. A mosaic is a picture or pattern made up of small components, such as stone or glass, or in this case, pixels.

Detective Kwan wants to *requisition*—or request—a chopper so she can be at the scene when the authorities apprehend the van.

Wire uses probability programs to try to guess where the most likely place of *apprehension* of the criminals will be. Apprehension in this context means taken into custody or arrested.

Detective Kwan is reluctant to let Ken come along in the chopper because of *liability* issues that have come up in other cases. She knows that the police department will be held accountable or responsible if anything happens to Ken.

The pilot of the chopper tells the passengers that they are traveling at about two hundred *knots* per hour. A knot is a unit of speed applied to planes, ships, and wind.

Detective Kwan reminds Ken to wait until the *rotors* stop before getting out of the helicopter. Rotors are the rotating blades on the helicopter that help it to take off and move through the air.

Forensic Techniques Used in CSC Case #11

Forensic Math Techniques

Two-Dimensional Calculus

Calculus is the mathematical study of change. It allows you to find maximum and minimum values. Integral calculus applies this study to two dimensions, and graphs them on a chart with x coordinates along a horizontal axis and y coordinates on the perpendicular axis. An example would be determining distance when the speed changes.

Real-Valued Function

In mathematics, a real-valued function is always a number that is contained within any of the infinite points along a number line.

Segmentation Techniques

When forensic mathematicians apply their field of study to photographs, they can sometimes add clarity to a fuzzy or indistinct image. In the analysis of objects in images, forensic mathematicians first need to distinguish between the objects of interest and the rest of the image, what is often grouped together as the background. The techniques that are used to find the

4.1 Calculus is the study of change. The nautilus shell (shown here in cross-section) is an example from nature of exponential growth and logarithmic spirals that are studied in calculus.

4.2 After a robbery, police might use computers to enhance video or photographs from the crime scene. However, if the images are enhanced too much, they will be too blurry to give any good evidence.

objects of interest are usually referred to as *segmentation techniques*, segmenting the foreground from background. Two of the most common techniques for doing this are called "thresholding" (which involves the brightness of objects or the contrast between dark and light) and edge finding, allowing outlines of objects to be determined. No single segmentation technique works for all images, and no segmentation technique is perfect—but these techniques allow forensics scientists to made "good guesses."

Computer-Enhanced Photographs

Computers allow forensic investigators to perform these procedures more quickly, efficiently, and accurately. That's one reason why computers are more important than ever in today's forensic field,. When it comes to images and video evidence, computers are used almost every step of the way. Investigators use computer software to get a better view of criminals, or the crime itself, In this chapter, Wire talks about increasing the number of pixels to clarify the details of the image. This is the same process investigators can use to catch criminals by enhancing images. The total number of pixels that can be viewed in an image is called the resolution. The higher the resolution, the clearer the picture. As Wire says, however, enlarge the image too much and it will

4.3 Video footage from surveillance cameras is not often clear enough to use as evidence in court. Video forensics experts can use computers to improve the quality of the footage to identify a suspect or for use in courtrooms.

become distorted. To remedy this problem, computer experts must use powerful software to convert security camera footage, or photographs containing evidence, into clear, reliable evidence. This new field of forensics is called video forensics, and is increasingly important in the realm of criminal investigation.

Who Is Dr. Leonid Rudin?

Dr. Leonid I. Rudin is the co-founder and CEO of Cognitech, Inc., an image-processing company based in Pasadena, California. Cognitech, founded in 1988, specializes in image and video software that assists in forensic investigations. Allowing investigators to enhance footage from a security camera to get a better look at the face of a criminal or the numbers on a license plate are prime examples of the business Cognitech and Dr. Rudin have been doing for years. Rudin was even asked by the Discovery Channel to verify a video that supposedly contained footage of UFOs in 1998. Cognitech and Dr. Rudin develop the advanced computer software investigators need to analyze images and videos that can be used to further the investigation or serve as evidence. This kind of software is quite important in the modern world of forensics.

CHAPTER 5

Evidence List

Vocab Words

chafed
pyre
quarry
inexorably

Deciphering the Evidence

When Ken was not allowed to accompany Detective Kwan and the police officers at the motel, he *chafed* inwardly. Chafe means to irritate or vex.

As Bonnie flees the burning vehicle, Jessa realizes that if she doesn't get out, the van will turn into a funeral *pyre*. A pyre is material that has been piled up for the purpose of burning a dead body.

After escaping from the van, Jessa glances back to see it balancing precariously over the edge of an immense *quarry*. A quarry is a large pit from which stone for building is dug out.

After rescuing Jessa, Ken slips down onto the van, which *inexorably* lurches forward and slides down the hillside. Inexorably means unrelentingly or without stopping.

120

Forensic Math in Court

Forensic mathematics isn't only useful to crime scene investigators; it's also helpful in the courtroom, where specialists in this field can guide judges and jurors regarding

5.1 Forensic mathematics and statistical analysis will often be used during criminal trials in a courtroom, especially in cases involving DNA analysis.

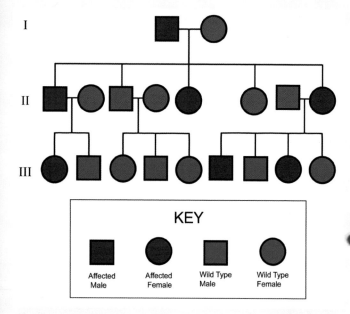

KEY

| Affected Male | Affected Female | Wild Type Male | Wild Type Female |

5.2 Statistical analysis is often used in the courtroom when a case involves DNA analysis, whether the question is about identity, paternity or another genetic relationship.

the possibility (or statistical probability) of an accused being an actual criminal. These techniques are often applied to questions having to do with genetics.

If type B blood was found at the scene of a crime, for example, and the accused person has type B blood, the mathematician can show the court the probability that the suspect is the murderer. In this case, in the general population, 1 person out of 12 has type B blood, so the odds are pretty high that someone else besides the accused could have committed the crime.

In another example, an abducted newborn baby was recovered, but the kidnappers claimed the baby was their own child. However, the alleged father had type A blood, the mother had type AB blood, and the baby had O blood. Meanwhile, the other set of parents (the ones whose child had been kidnapped) have type A and type B blood. Probability analysis proves that there is zero probability that the baby is the biological offspring of the accused kidnappers, but there is a 1/2 probability that the mother with the missing child is the biological mother.

CHAPTER 6

Evidence List

Vocab Words

delirium
medicine man
pawns
interrogated
prosthetic

Deciphering the Evidence

Ken doesn't know how long he has been lost in a *delirium* of painkillers. The drugs have caused him to have severe mental confusion and disturbance about where he is and what has happened.

Jessa tells Ken that Mr. Peshlaki, the *medicine man*—or Native American healer— had performed a ceremony for him using corn pollen.

Jessa explains to Ken that the rest of Bonnie and Dylan's sales crew were *pawns* in the operation. Pawns are people used by others for their own purpose.

Jessa goes on to tell Ken that the police *interrogated* Bonnie and Dylan, but didn't get any answers. To interrogate is to ask questions in a formal way.

Ken tells Jessa that his hand won't be any better than a *prosthetic* one. Prosthetic refers to an artificial replacement (prosthesis) for a part of the body that has been lost or injured.

Why Do the Diné People Believe That Corn Pollen Has Healing Properties?

Corn pollen is considered by the Diné people to be pure and life-sustaining. In the Navajo belief system, corn pollen symbolizes the renewal of life and is thought to restore the harmony that is lost when a person is ill.

6.1 Diné, or Navajo, people believe that corn pollen can restore lost harmony to a sick person's life.

What Is the "Good-Cop–Bad-Cop" Approach to Interrogation?

This is a psychological tactic used for interrogation, where a team of two interrogators take apparently opposing attitudes to the person being questioned. The interrogators may interview the subject alternately or may confront the subject at the same time, but in either case, the "bad cop" takes an aggressive, negative stance towards the subject, making blatant accusations, insulting comments, threats, and making the person being questioned generally dislike him or her. This sets the stage for the "good cop" to act sympathetically by appearing supportive, understanding, and "nice." The good cop will also seem to defend the person being questioned from the bad cop. This tends to make the person feel he or she can cooperate with the good cop and confide the needed information.

Forensic Math Techniques

More About Algorithms

An example is Euclid's algorithm to determine the maximum common divisor of two integers greater than one: "subtract the smallest number from the biggest

6.2 Euclid, a Greek mathematician in about 300 BCE, is known as the father of geometry.

one, repeat until you get a zero or a one." The number of subtractions needed is always smaller than the biggest of the two numbers.

Computers are often used for carrying out algorithms. As Boolos and Jeffrey (two famous mathematicians) explain:

No human being can write fast enough, or long enough, or small enough to list all members of an innumerably infinite set by writing out their names, one after another, in some notation. But humans can do something equally useful, in the case of certain innumerably infinite sets: They can give explicit instructions for determining the nth member of the set, for arbitrary finite n. Such instructions are to be given quite explicitly, in a form in which they could be followed by a computing machine, or by a human who is capable of carrying out only very elementary operations on symbols

Wrapping CSC Case #11

As Ken says, this Crime Scene Case was pretty much solved "by the numbers." In other words, Wire's math and probability equations were more useful than any of the more dramatic techniques sometimes used in crime solving. Given Ken's circumstances, this is especially comforting to him: it means that despite the fact that his body's new limitations may prevent him from more "active duty," there are plenty of other ways that he can still solve crimes. Using logic and intelligence; paying attention to details; and applying math, science, and computer skills are the most effective ways to solve crimes.

Wire is able to apply mathematics and probability analysis to help locate Jessa, to crack Bonnie and Dylan's code and to convince Dylan to confess. These are all valid applications of math to forensics. However, one of the most common applications of forensics mathematics is in cases of DNA analysis, to determine the probability of an individual's identity based on DNA test results.

Deoxyribonucleic acid, DNA for short, is the genetic code within the cells of a living organism that guides the development and function of an organism's life. Human DNA is composed of about 3 billion bases, about 99 percent of which are the same in all people. In 1985, an English geneticist named Dr. Alec Jeffreys discovered that certain regions of these bases were composed

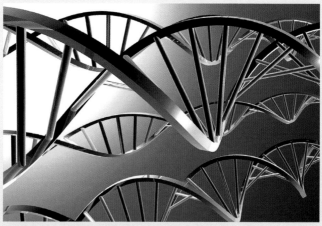

Strands of DNA showing the double helix structure.

A molecular chemist preparing a DNA sample for analysis.

of sequences repeated multiple times right next to each other. The length of these repeat regions (called variable number of tandem repeats or VNTRs) varies from individual to individual. By studying the length of the VNTRs it was possible to perform identity tests with DNA. The technique used to study the VNTRs is known as restriction fragment length polymorphism (RFLP) because a chemical called a restriction enzyme is used to cut the pieces of DNA surrounding the VNTRs.

This image shows gel electrophoresis, during which an electric current moves a DNA sample through an agarose gel causing the sample to separate out into its components.

Since the development of RFLP, the use of DNA analysis has become widespread as part of crime scene investigations. However, RFLP requires a large sample of DNA in order to complete the analysis accurately. Dr. Kary Mullis solved this problem with the development of the polymerase chain reaction (PCR), which takes a tiny fragment of DNA and copies it many times in a test tube. Using PCR, within a couple of hours a few DNA molecules can become a billion molecules. The invention of PCR allowed other DNA analysis techniques to gain importance in crime scene investigation.

Short tandem repeat (STR) analysis is the most widely used method today because STRs are shorter in length and degradation is not as much of a concern as it is for the longer VNTRs needed in RFLP analysis. STRs are repeats of three to seven base pairs found commonly throughout an individual's DNA. Each place (locus) where the repeats occur only has a few variations between all individuals, but comparing several at once gives a DNA signature. In the United States, the FBI has selected thirteen specific loci as the standard for this signature. This standard of thirteen loci is stored in the FBI's Combined DNA Indexing System (CODIS), which is a database that the FBI uses to share and compare DNA signature results.

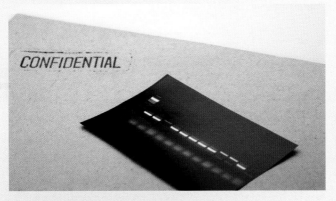

After gel electrophoresis is complete, a picture (shown here) is taken of the separated DNA sample. This can then be compared to other analyzed DNA samples, to test for an identity match.

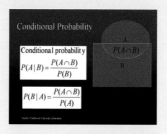

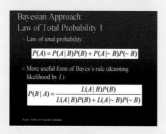

Ken struggles through his forensic mathematics classes at NAU, and he feels frustrated by the ease with which Wire handles all the difficult statistical equations. Ken is not alone—many students struggle with math. These forensic notes have tried to simplify complicated concepts with clear explanations and examples. However, for those like Wire who can handle the real math, here are some of the equations behind Bayesian statistical analysis.

Bayesian Approach:
Law of Total Probability 2

- Law of total probability:

$$P(A) = \sum_{\text{all } j} P(A \mid B_j) P(B_j)$$

- Even more useful form of Bayes's rule:

$$P(B_i \mid A) = \frac{L(A \mid B_i) P(B_i)}{\sum_{\text{all } j} L(A \mid B_j) P(B_j)}$$

Pacific Northwest National Laboratory

Bayesian Approach:
The Prior Probability 1

$$P(B_i \mid A) = \frac{L(A \mid B_i) P(B_i)}{\sum_{\text{all } j} L(A \mid B_j) \, P(\quad_j)}$$

- Some form of prior probability is required!
- The prior probability is what you know before you start
- The prior can have more or less effect on the posterior, depending on the precision of the data
- The prior can be subjective
- The prior is the topic of unresolvable arguments

Pacific Northwest National Laboratory

Bayesian Approach:
The Prior Probability 2

$$P(B_i \mid A) = \frac{L(A \mid B_i) P(B_i)}{\sum_{\text{all } j} L(A \mid B_j) P(B_j)}$$

- The prior can be "nothing"
  - even "nothing" can take several forms
  - "uniform," "flat," or "uninformative" prior: all values of B are "equally probable"
  - "vague" prior: all values of $\ln(B)$ are equally probable.
- The prior can be hard to nail down
  - "small values of background are more likely than large ones"

Pacific Northwest National Laboratory

Philosophical Statement of Bayes's Rule

$$P(\text{state of nature} \mid \text{evidence}) = \frac{L(\text{evidence} \mid \text{state of nature}) \, P(\text{state of nature})}{\text{normalizing factor}}$$

- The "state of nature" (e.g., count rate from analyte) is what we want to know
- The "evidence" is what we have observed
- The likelihood of the "evidence" given the "state of nature" is what we know about the way nature works
- The probability of the state of nature is what we believed before we obtained the evidence

Pacific Northwest National Laboratory

FURTHER READING

Campbell, Andrea. *Forensic Science: Evidence, Clues, and Investigation*. Philadelphia, Penn.: Chelsea House Publishers, 2000.

Craig, Emily. T*easing Secrets from the Dead. My Investigations at America's Most Infamous Crime Scenes*. New York: Crown Publishers, 2004.

Evans , Colin. *The Casebook of Forensic Detection: How Science Solved 100 of the World's Most Baffling Crimes*. New York: John Wiley & Sons, 2006.

Innes, Brian. *Forensic Science*. Philadelphia, Penn.: Mason Crest Publishers, 2006.

Morton, James. *Catching the Killers: A History of Crime Detection*. London, England: Ebury Press, 2001.

FOR MORE INFORMATION

Brenner, Charles. World Trade Center Disaster Identification Diary. dna-view.com/wtcdiary.htm

Crime and Clues
www.crimeandclues.com/

Crime Library, "Forensic Files,"
www.trutv.com/shows/forensic_files/techniques/print.html

Forensics Mathematics. teach.fcps.net/immex/preview/Forensics/forensics1/index.htm

How Stuff Works, "How Crime Scene Investigation Works," www.howstuffworks.com/csi.htm

BIBLIOGRAPHY

Forensics Mathematics. DNA-review.com

Genge, N. E. *The Forensic Casebook*. New York: Ballantine Books, 2002.

Lyle, D.P. *Forensics for Dummies*. Indianapolis, Ind.: Wiley, 2004.

Owen, David. *Hidden Evidence. Forty True Crimes and How Forensic Science Helped Solved Them*. Buffalo, N.Y.: Firefly Books, 2000.

Wecht, Cyril H. *Crime Scene Investigation*. Pleasantville, N.Y.: The Reader's Digest Association, Inc, 2004.

INDEX

PICTURE CREDITS

BIOGRAPHIES

Author

Kenneth McIntosh is a freelance writer and college instructor who lives in beautiful Flagstaff, Arizona (while CSC is fictional, Flagstaff is definitely real). He has enjoyed crime fiction—from Sherlock Holmes to CSI and Bones—and is thankful for the opportunity to create his own detective stories. Now, if he could only find his car keys . . .

Ken would like to thank the following people:

Tom Oliver, who invented the title 'Crime Scene Club' on a tram en route to the Getty Museum, and cooked up the best plots while we sat at his Tiki bar . . . Mr. Levin's Creative Writing students at the Flagstaff Arts and Leadership Academy, *who vetted the books . . . Rob and Jenny Mullen and Victor Viera, my Writer's Group, who shared their lives and invaluable insights . . . My recently deceased father, Dr. A Vern McIntosh, who taught me when I was a child to love written words. This series could not have happened without all of you.*

Series Consultant

Carla Miller Noziglia is Senior Forensic Advisor, Tanzania, East Africa, for the U.S. Department of Justice, International Criminal Investigative Training Assistant Program. A Fellow of the American Academy of Forensic Sciences her work has earned her many honors and commendations, including Distinguished Fellow from the American Academy of Forensic Sciences (2003) and the Paul L.

Kirk Award from the American Academy of Forensic Sciences Criminalistics Section. Ms. Noziglia's publications include *The Real Crime Lab* (coeditor, 2005), *So You Want to be a Forensic Scientist* (coeditor 2003), and contributions to *Drug Facilitated Sexual Assault* (2001), *Convicted by Juries, Exonerated by Science: Case Studies in the Use of DNA* (1996), and the *Journal of Police Science* (1989).

Illustrator

John Ashton Golden is freelance illustrator, comics creator, and graphic designer living and working from his Chicago IL "Mortal Mirror Studio." When not at the drawing table or keeping cats off the computer, John enjoys bicycling, writing, playing songs for his band Metahumans, esoteric research, socializing, and spontaneous adventure.